Merlin's Apprentice: Warrior Rising

Susan McCauley

Celtic Sea Publishing

This book was published by Celtic Sea, LLC.

Text by Susan McCauley. Copyright © 2024 by Ex Libris, LLC. All Rights Reserved.

Cover art and design by Christian Bentulan. Copyright © 2024 by Ex Libris, LLC.

Map art by Cat Skully. Copyright © 2022.

All rights reserved under the International and PanAmerican Copyright Conventions. No part of this book may be reproduced, translated, or transmitted in any form or by any means, electronically or mechanical, including photocopying, recording, or by any information storage and retrieval system, without permission in writing from publisher.

The unauthorized reproduction or distribution of this copyrighted work is illegal.

Publisher: Celtic Sea Publishing. www.celticseallc.com

ISBN: 978-1-951069-24-7 (hardcover)

ISBN: 978-1-951069-25-4 (paperback)

ISBN: 978-1-951069-26-1 (e-book)

Part One
Invaders

One

Icy black waves rose and fell, breaking against a barbaric wooden prow that sliced through the frigid waters.

"What do you see?" A woman's soft voice whispered in Pip's ear, auburn wisps of her hair tickling his nose along with her scent of herbs and smoke.

"I–I don't know." He stared into the whirling fog of the cauldron, trying to see more clearly. Whatever was there, he sensed danger.

"Look closely," she coaxed. "Look into the mist. See beyond it."

Pip forced his drowsy lids to stay open. He let them glaze like ice as he stared into Caraline's roiling brew. "I see . . . I see waves. Dark and light, crashing against a ship . . . I can taste the salt on my lips."

"Look closer. Closer." Her gentle fingers pressed Pip's head forward, steam and mist swirling like intoxicating fumes into his nostrils.

He gazed into the cold blackness of the sea, then let his eyes wander up the prow that was carved with a great dragon-like beast rising from the water. He pulled back, allowing himself to float, weightless, like a gull in the breeze.

Huge blood-red square sails snapped taut, and wild-looking men rowed, their oars dipping simultaneously into the water. Large, circular shields hung against the outside of the ship, making the vessel itself look ready for battle. The men were bearded, with light hair, bright blue eyes, and cheeks ruddy from the wind. Their muscles were large and lean. They laughed and sang and chatted. Their tongue sounded strange, the words foreign.

"Ships," Pip coughed, pulling himself from the mist and away from Caraline. "Strange ships with large sails and prows carved like monsters. Sailed by savage-looking men with shields."

The slim woman collapsed into a nearby chair, her brow furrowing into a worried frown, but she kept the purple brew of the cauldron swirling with a flick of her wrist. "It is as I feared."

"Why should you fear ships and strange men on the sea?" Pip glanced through the arrow slit window of the castle tower where he spent much of his time studying herbs and potions with Caraline and watched the battle mages training in the yard below.

After his family had left, Pip had loved to train with Bowan and the soldiers. His family had been gone only a few months, but the pain of their absence was still fresh like a wound on his soul, and Pip's training the only remedy. The harder he fought, the more he pushed his body and the less he felt the pain of losing them. Except he couldn't find the right weapon. The bow he'd once used for sport, the one he'd so longed to dash through the woods with in the excitement of the hunt, was no longer fun. The bow. His old friend. Now it seemed a tool for death. And the sword he'd been given, nothing more than a clumsy extension of his arm. Since his family had gone and he'd become a mage at Imbolc, the spring solstice, nothing seemed to feel as it should.

Caraline's green-eyed gaze pierced Pip's shoulder blades, returning him to the present and making him shiver. "I fear them because they are headed for our shores."

Pip stared again into the cauldron, wishing an answer would appear. "Our shores? Are you certain?"

"I am. North. Near our old homes."

Pip fought the chill that crept down his spine, along his arms, and into his heart. "This is my home now." The village where he'd been born and raised was nothing but a memory. Just as his family was nothing but a memory. They were gone. Sent to a new world, a new realm. He'd been left here because of his magic, and he wore the red sash of a full mage to prove it. All that he had left of his family now was his name: Phillip Gwynhoed. Pip. And he had Alfred, he supposed. Alfred was a friend. The angel-faced magus scribe had stayed behind to help him and Merlin make something of this new world they'd created by sending the ordinarius, the non-magical, to a realm of their own.

And Caraline was here, too. That was good. She was loving and calming and full of light. She'd come south from Aquae Sulis not long after the breaking of the Earth Realm and the Magic Realm, as Merlin called them. With her herbs and brews and soft words, she helped Pip focus on his ability of sight so he could see what others could not so easily ascertain.

Caraline rose, smoothed the green sash at her waist that marked her as a magus, as a person born with power, but not a mage, and went to the door. "Merlin will no doubt want to hear of this, and I must prepare for our guest." Her face lit with a smile at the last word.

"Our guest?" Pip asked. He didn't know they were having a guest.

"My niece." Caraline smiled as if she held a wonderful secret. "The one from the north I've told you about."

"Your niece?" Pip gulped. He'd forgotten Caraline still had family here after their world had been torn apart.

"Gwenn. She's about your age. Quite keen on magic and a powerful magus. I hope Master Merlin will train her."

"But girls aren't permitted to train as mages, are they?" Pip asked. At least he'd seen no apprentices who were girls, or any female mages, for that matter.

"Not yet," Caraline said, her lips forming an unhappy line. "I'm hoping he'll train her, nonetheless. I sent word to her before I left Aquae Sulis to meet me here. But I've yet to hear from her, and I fear she did not receive my missive." She wrung her hands for a moment, then murmured a word that immediately put out the fire beneath the cauldron. A fine twist of smoke reached toward the open window. "Her mother, my sister, was not magus. Nor was Gwenn's father."

"So they left her," Pip blurted out, feeling a hollow in his chest that this girl he didn't know had been abandoned as he had been. Not that it was her parents' fault. It wasn't. It was his and Merlin's and King Arthur's fault for tearing the world in two.

Caraline wrapped her arm around Pip's shoulder and gave him an affectionate squeeze. "I know it's painful. But she was not abandoned, Pip. She understands, like you do, why the ordinarius had to be spared from our world. She didn't want to see her family enslaved any more than you did yours. Besides, she has me and Merlin. And you and Alfred, too, if you'll accept her."

Pip grimaced, and his stomach twisted in knots. The last thing he wanted was more trouble. And from the way the soldiers talked, girls were trouble. He'd just found a friend in Alfred, and he could barely think of his little sister, Mary, without a stone of sadness filling his gut. And now he was expected to befriend a strange girl? He wasn't sure he was ready to let someone new into his heart.

Twenty mages gathered in the circular room that had once been home to King Arthur and his knights. Stone walls encased the circular room, which was aglow from the thick tallow candles that flickered and issued tendrils of dark smoke from a large wrought iron chandelier hanging above the round table. The tall, arched windows were spaced evenly around the room, allowing in the afternoon light. Some were open to let in the summer breeze and let out the stench of burning tallow. A few were shuttered. Between the windows, affixed to the stone, were flickering torches held in place by newly installed decorative iron sconces with the emblem of Britain, as the new Magic Realm of Britannia was being called. The emblem was a triskele—the same tattoo-like scar that emblazoned Pip's palm.

A raven with mischievous black eyes perched on a sunny windowsill, eyeing Pip with interest. From his pocket, Pip scooped the crust of bread he'd saved from his last meal, broke it into bits, and sprinkled them on the window ledge. "Here you go," he said, smiling at the bird. The ravens were his friends and had been ever since they'd helped him and King Arthur defeat Mordred. He tried to give them treats whenever he saw them.

Tap. Tap. Tap.

Merlin pounded the base of his rowan wood staff against the stone floor. The sound echoed throughout the chamber, calling everyone to attention. The great mage sat in an intricately carved oak chair, a relic of the majesty of King Arthur's court. Merlin's cool blue eyes assessed the newly formed Aurelian Council of Mages, who sat at the massive round table where the most important of Arthur's knights and advisors had once met. The Aurelian Council, headed by Merlin, consisted of full mages. Their intent was to keep the southern kingdom in order until a new king could be appointed. Merlin intended for the council to serve the yet-to-be-named king.

Pip settled into place at Merlin's left with Caraline beside him. Alfred sat at Merlin's right, acting as the official scribe. Pip still cringed that he had been placed so close to Merlin in such a position of honor. He was not a great mage, merely a boy newly inducted into the great Order of Mages because of circumstances and inherited power. He glanced around the room, studying the colorful auras that swirled around the head of each mage.

All wore cloaks of blacks and browns, and each member wore a red sash with colored runes that spoke to their power of mastery. Weather mages had metallic blue runes etched onto their red sashes, artisan mages had brown runes as they often worked with wood and metals from the earth, and earth mages had pale green runes. Pip thought he'd obtain the orange rune of the fire mage and, possibly, if Bowan had his way, the gold rune of the battle mage, but he hadn't mastered either yet. Very few mages bore the coveted silver rune, which marked them as a master mage: a mage who excelled in three or more areas of magic. Pip had only ever met one such mage: Merlin.

Aside from their clothing, each mage had halos of varying colors. Some had shades of green, others oranges, blues, reds, and pinks. Pip was still learning, but the auras seemed to represent each mage's type of power. Those with lots of green in their auras, like Caraline, were inclined to work with herbs and earth magic. Those with lots of blues seemed to be fond of manipulating the weather. And those with reds and oranges were often gifted in fire and battle magic. Merlin's aura was a deep, luminous purple, and he seemed to be good at many types of magic. Pip had gotten used to seeing auras since he'd come fully into his power, but so many powerful ones in a single place were a bit distracting. The room seemed to swell with magic.

Merlin's aura flared slightly, and he cleared his throat, waiting for silence. A weather mage with a blue and brown aura whom Pip barely knew mumbled something that Pip couldn't understand.

"Is there a problem, Faelen?" Merlin's voice was soft but powerful.

An elder weather mage, Faelen, with sagging jowls, liver-spotted arms, and a scraggly beard, looked from Caraline, then back to Merlin. "She is a woman and not a full mage. She's not one of us. How can you have her sit with the council?" Faelen croaked.

Caraline's emerald green aura flared, then quickly settled when Merlin spoke.

"The *woman's* name is Caraline. And while we've not yet admitted a female to the Order of Mages, I see no reason why we should not. She is not only a lady but also has more skill than some of you." A few mages grumbled at Merlin's words, but most nodded approvingly. "Lady Caraline is a powerful magus and a trusted friend. We shall see to it that she is made a full mage and inducted into the Order of Mages and, in time, that she becomes a member of the Aurelian Council, but for the moment she is here as my personal council. Now, there is urgent business."

Faelen opened his mouth again, but Merlin's glare made him snap it shut like a flytrap clamping down on its prey.

The weight of Merlin's gaze ensured all were silent before he continued. "Where Mordred once ruled the north, there is now a void. The dark mages of the wilds are returning home, and with them any who believed in the path Mordred had set before them. Although they lack organization and can no longer have ordinarius to enslave, they can pursue their dark arts. And we cannot—we must not—allow that to happen."

A murmur of ascent rose within the chamber, the mages' auras blazing with color as their tempers flared, Pip's included. He certainly didn't want another Mordred rising from the ashes of the corpse-strewn battlefields of Badon and beyond.

"With King Arthur and so many of our leaders sent to the Earth Realm, there is no leadership across the land," Merlin said. "And our remaining magi-soldiers have brought news that many farms lay unsown, homes are abandoned, and shops remain empty."

"With no spring planting, there will be nothing to harvest. We will surely starve come next winter." An old mage spoke—one Pip knew was a farmer who had used his powers to enhance his crops.

"We will consider putting you in charge of the magus who choose to work the land. But necessity may prove that some who don't want to farm must do so," said Merlin, looking around the table, seeking willing volunteers. "There will be many jobs that used to fall to the ordinarius that the magus and mages must do."

"And what of our army? And Mordred's schools of dark magic? Won't the surviving mages loyal to Mordred try to resume their treacherous teachings?" Faelen asked.

"We must restore order, and we will," Merlin said. "We must assess how many dark mages remain loyal to Mordred's ideals and how many we can persuade to the light."

"Our remaining holy men should be dispatched to set up monasteries across the countryside. This will ensure that God's word survives the chaos," said Alfred, speaking with so much authority that Pip had to look twice to make sure it was really Angel Face who'd spoken.

"And what about the old gods?" asked Caraline.

"Yes! Will we let the old ways die out for the new?" Faelen growled, his words trampling Caraline's soft voice. At least Faelen agreed with Caraline on something, Pip thought.

Alfred cowered slightly, but watched the mage, which Pip now realized Caraline was: a mage—even if she didn't hold the title. When he'd first met her in Aquae Sulis, he'd thought she was a simple magus medicine woman, a purveyor of herbs. But Merlin was right. She was much more than a talented magus, and he wondered why Merlin hadn't brought Caraline into the Order of Mages before now. True, there were no female mages, but that didn't mean there shouldn't be. Their power and their gifts would be a boon to the Order of Mages, to Britain, and to the realm.

"Perhaps we can coexist," Caraline said, her calm voice bringing a sense of serenity over the room. She tilted her head in understanding to Faelen, but smiled at Alfred to continue.

Alfred leaned away from Faelen, but went on, his voice firm. "Of course we can coexist."

Faelen lurched forward, a hiss of thunder escaping his gnarled, snaggled teeth and spittle catching on the weave of his facial hair.

Merlin held up a hand for peace. "Christianity will continue, but the old ways will not die, Faelen. They will endure, as we have . . . Perhaps not in the same form as we have known for so many centuries, but they will endure." He looked at each face, willing each to look him in the eye. "Change is hard. But we will survive."

"And what of the invaders?" Pip squeaked, surprised to hear himself voice his concern before an audience of elder mages.

"Invaders?" Merlin's gaze narrowed. The purple halo that surrounded him darkened.

Caraline pursed her lips and frowned. "Aye, Lord Merlin. Our old and barbaric ways may still have some use," she said, then took a deep breath before continuing. "Invaders are coming. Savage Northmen. Ready to fight for new lands. Ready to bring their magic and their gods to our home."

Several alarmed voices broke out around the table.

"Why didn't you bring this to my attention immediately?" Merlin's forehead creased.

"We only discovered it this morning. Pip used his sight and confirmed the warnings I saw in my runes. They are already sailing their wooden ships toward our shores," Caraline said, watching the raven who had finished the last of his crumbs launch himself from his sunny perch into the bright blue sky. "And because I am not a mage or a member of the Aurelian Council, I thought it best to hold my tongue until we were alone." Faelen glared, and Merlin merely looked thoughtful.

"Well, you're quite right to bring it up to the council," said a kind-looking mage with wrinkled skin and blue eyes. "It is now imperative that we send scouts and soldiers north to secure the new kingdom."

"Yes, and even more reason to establish monasteries," said Bowan, which surprised Pip. Bowan wasn't openly Christian or druid. "We can post soldiers at each school and holy center, and set up a way for information on dark mage activity and invasions to be relayed to us quickly in the south." Bowan represented the magi-soldiers and oversaw the security of the new kingdom.

"It sounds more like we'll be establishing new towns," said one tired-looking mage.

"Or re-inhabiting old ones," said Caraline. "We can use what already exists and build what we need."

"We may need to move our seat to Winchester. There is already a stone fort there. Stronger than this, and with better access to the river," Merlin said. "We can build monastic compounds across the Kingdom of Britain, with schools attached to teach our ways and those of the Christians. Children will be schooled in religions and magic. The soldiers can have barracks nearby, but not within the schools or holy places."

Faelen and Alfred nodded. Pip silently agreed as well. It wouldn't do for soldiers to bring their crude behavior and vulgar stories and unsavory women into such places. Still, if they were close enough to the monasteries and schools, they'd offer protection to the magi-priests, students, and the towns and nearby villages.

"We can assume possession of Mordred's school for mages in Etin and make it a school of light. It will be the northern most outpost before the Wilds. We'll send others to do the same in Aquae Sulis, Lundein, Mamucium, Eoforwīc, Pons Aelius, Winchester, and Eidyn. But we must establish a foothold quickly before Mordred's surviving mages resume their dark works." Merlin tapped his steepled fingers. "We have secured the lands to the south, and it may take years to form these schools. However, we must assess the lands to the north and discover those who remain as our enemies. I will hold further council with my advisors. Let's reconvene in the morning with a plan. Bowan, prepare the men. A journey awaits."

Two

"Don't drop your guard," Niall barked, his thick, muscled arms tense and ready to strike. His cloak was tossed to the side, as was his green sash marked with the pale golden runes of a magus-soldier, leaving him clothed only in a sleeveless tunic and trousers. Sweat dripped from his brow, and he tossed his sword from one hand to the other. "Too much lazing around with cauldrons and potions. You must still be able to fight. And even I can see your aura. You must work on keeping it dimmed when you don't want to be seen."

Pip's arm sagged under the weight of the sword, but he forced himself to stand tall. At least Niall and Bowan hadn't been sent to the Earth Realm. Bowan was a powerful battle mage, and Niall was the best magus-soldier in Britain. With a wealth of battle experience, they could lead and train the new magi-soldiers and battle mages. Pip was happy to be a magus-soldier for now. He could fight and follow command, but he definitely didn't have the skills of a battle mage. Battle mages were something different entirely. It took an immense amount of power and control to be a full battle mage, and Pip wasn't sure he'd ever achieve the title. He still didn't know where he fit in this new world of mages or who he was to become. He'd fought before, but that was out of rage against Mordred and all the evil he'd stood for.

Now he felt aimless. There was all the training with swords and potions and spells, but no proper mission. As much as he loved his new home in Merlin's tower in South Cadbury, he itched for the freedom of adventure.

"Oh, for Merlin's sake, lad! Your aura is like a rainbow, your mind drifting. At least try to use your sword." Niall raised his sword again and charged.

Pip couldn't see his own aura, but he knew it must match his swirling thoughts. He needed to work more on masking his aura. The ability to hide one's aura during battle was essential to winning a fight, but it was so much work, and he wasn't ready to face a new enemy.

Niall thrust forward, and Pip parried but did not engage. "It just doesn't feel right." He dipped the sword so the tip nearly touched the dirt. "Nothing feels right . . . Ever since the battle . . . ever since Galen . . ." Ever since he'd nearly killed his brother and almost cost King Arthur his life, the sword hadn't felt right. It was heavy. Awkward. Wrong. "None of it feels right. Not even my bow. I don't feel like Phillip Gwynhoed, the first full mage of the new Kingdom of Britain."

"Well, what do you feel like?"

He shrugged and thought for a moment. "Just Pip." A fledgling mage in a new and troubled world who longed to run through the woods without a care.

Niall sheathed his sword and bit his lower lip. "I wonder . . ." He scratched at the scruff on his chin.

"What?"

It was Niall's turn to shrug. "Time. You just need time . . . more training and time. The heaviness you feel will ease." He slapped Pip's back in a way that shook him to the marrow of his bones. "Or perhaps you will find a great new weapon in battle!" He chuckled, but Pip wasn't sure he was ready to see battle again, at least not soon. Training to protect the kingdom was one thing, but fighting and killing was something else entirely.

Before Niall could begin another bout with the sword, Caraline swept gracefully toward them from Merlin's tower. The soldiers whispered of Caraline's power; they murmured she was more than a healer. Pip knew she had magic. He'd felt it. But he hadn't realized how powerful she was until the war with Mordred had ended and he'd been able to study her aura. When she was happy, as she was now, it was green and brown with sparkles of shimmering gold.

"Pip, lad." She smiled warmly and extended a hand. "Come. Merlin is asking for you."

Pip gratefully positioned the handle of his sword toward Niall, who took the weapon from him with a narrow-eyed scowl. "We'll train more tomorrow. Now go along, and I'll see to these," Niall said of the practice swords. "Just be sure to keep your guard up. And practice!"

Caraline fondly linked arms with Pip, bringing him back to the swirling sounds and smells and auras of the people and animals filling the courtyard. Stone walls loomed above them as they entered a tower and took the twisting staircase toward Arthur's old chambers, now Merlin's private meeting rooms.

Merlin's owl hooted as they entered, and Pip went over to scratch his feathered friend beneath the chin. Alfred glared. The owl had never seemed fond of Alfred and pecked at the boy's quills when Alfred wasn't looking. It made Merlin and Pip laugh, but Alfred would mumble under his breath about not trusting owls.

"Caraline. Pip." Merlin nodded them to two empty seats at the table.

Pip sat beside Alfred, and Caraline beside Bowan. It was a small group of those who had become Merlin's most trusted advisors.

"I trust your training is going well," Bowan said, looking Pip dead in the eye until he squirmed.

"It's . . . going," Pip said. "I—can't find the right sword."

"We'll discuss your training later," Merlin said. "There are things of greater importance that we must discuss now." He gestured to a parchment map of Britain that lay on the table before them. The map showed their entire island with small castles drawn in to denote fortresses, like Arthur's old castle in South Cadbury and Mordred's old fortress near Eidyn.

Alfred hunched over the map, studying it. His fingers were cloaked in ink, and just below the town named Eidyn, he wrote the place name Etin.

"What are you doing?" Pip asked, leaning closer so he could get a better view of the map.

"Updating place names. The Roman names are dying out, and other names are changing, too, in how they're spoken. You see here." Alfred pointed to the word Albion. "*Albion* is what our island has been called for centuries, but some refer to it as Britain. So I've got both place names marked. And here," Alfred said, pointing to the city of Eidyn. "We no longer say Eidyn, we say Etin. So I've made a notation to reflect that change."

He tapped the map farther south to the place named Wintancaester. "Most of us call this Winchester now." In his neat, steady hand, Alfred wrote the word Winchester on the map beneath Wintancaester. "I'm just trying to keep the map current. Once the kingdom is more settled, I'll make a whole new map. But that could take years." Excitement laced his voice, but Pip felt a bit sick. The thought of having to study and remember all those names and places and history was overwhelming.

"To the matter at hand." The power in Merlin's voice sliced through the room, making everyone look up. "Bowan and I have talked long through the night, and we are agreed on some strategic plans. The first is that we must form an army to go north. We must ensure Mordred's schools and fortress are entrusted to those of the light and not his dark ways. Pip, I want you, Alfred, and Caraline to go back north with me to Etin. Then we can discover more about these invaders you have seen. We must determine if they've landed on our shores."

Pip's stomach dropped. Etin. All the way back north. He was ready for an adventure, but going to Etin could take weeks, and that was if they didn't come across any of Mordred's dark mages. That could be real trouble. Trouble he wasn't ready to fight.

"I'd rather stay here." His voice sounded soft but certain. "To study spells and to work on magic. And I need more practice with my sword."

"I guessed what you would prefer. I'd prefer the same." Merlin stood with a groan. "These old bones would prefer a nice feather bed in a warm castle to a thin pallet on the cold roadside. But this is not a time for what we *want* to do, it's what we *must* do for the sake of the kingdom. And we must stomp out the darkness and secure these lands. We must not let our kingdom continue without guidance."

Merlin was always so practical. Of course they couldn't do what they wanted, but that didn't mean Pip didn't want to scream his opposition. What if he faced another dark mage and someone else he loved got killed?

"And there's the matter of the invaders you scried," said Bowan, looking to Pip. He drummed his fingers on the map. "I've heard rumors about them from soldiers who've spent time at sea. Rumors of fierce warriors from the north. Northmen, they're called."

"The runes predicted they were not to invade for centuries, but the future of the world was altered when you and Merlin broke our realms from one another. They're arriving early." Caraline's voice was sharp, her eyes flecked with unusual concern. "They are savage warriors, as Bowan has said. And they bring with them dark magic and their own gods."

Merlin shook his head. "We cannot ignore what is coming to our shores any more than we can ignore the void of leadership in our lands. We cannot afford to let these invaders fill that void. Just imagine a ruler worse than Mordred."

"Worse than Mordred?" Alfred gulped.

"To ignore them would breed more chaos. More death . . ." said Caraline. "Powerful mages, those filled with *draoidheachd*, must travel north with our army to stop them."

Pip shifted uncomfortably. He could scarcely imagine a ruler worse than Mordred. Someone who had been willing to steal children from their families if they didn't have magic. He'd torn apart the very soul of their realm. Pip wouldn't let that happen. Never again. But he wasn't a battle mage. Not yet.

"There are still plenty of mages here. Battle mages even. Why must I go?" Pip asked Caraline.

"You know the north better than any of us," Merlin said simply. "And though you are still young, your power is vast."

"There will be great darkness on this path, Merlin." Caraline's voice held a note of fear. "I've seen it in the runes."

"Don't worry about Pip or Alfred, Caraline. We will be with them. As for your niece, we will stop in Aquae Sulis on the way north to inquire about her and see how the city fares in these changing times," said Merlin.

Caraline's gaze fell to the floor, her eyes glimmering with tears.

Merlin's voice softened as though he understood how hard it must be to take her niece on such a dangerous mission. "We'll find her. We'll teach her, along with Pip and Alfred." Merlin sighed a deep, tired sigh. "With Mordred gone, we have more to concern ourselves with than our northern lands and these invaders from the sea."

"More?" Caraline asked. "The runes have shown me nothing else."

"I have eyes and ears in many places. And they tell me that the powers within the old wall waiver. *Things*," he said, his glance darting to Bowan, then back to Caraline, "are beginning to come through."

"What sorts of 'things'?" Pip asked.

"Things of darkness, things of light. Things not of this realm or of the Earth Realm. Things of the Realm of Faerie."

"Faerie? They're merely myths and legends." Alfred snorted, then stopped short when he saw the serious glint in Merlin's eyes. Alfred swallowed hard. "You mean things like elves and goblins are real?"

Merlin nodded. "Long before the Romans invaded, the creatures of Faerie had a hold on this land, and all our forests were mystical and enchanted. When the Romans came, they pushed most of the creatures back to their own realm and held them there with the power imbued within Hadrian's Wall."

"But Hadrian's Wall was built to keep the Caledonians out of Roman territory," Alfred said, sounding unsure of how one of his many facts could be incorrect.

Merlin nodded. "Yes, the people of the north—the barbarians, as the Romans called them—lived deep in the Caledonian Forest. But there were others there, too. The elves and goblins, trolls, and even dragons. And those creatures are the ones the Romans forced into the Realm of Faerie, which they blocked with the power in the wall itself. We access the northern lands through gates in the wall, but beyond the wall itself is another realm."

"You mean Hadrian's Wall is not simply a physical barrier, but also a barrier between the Magic Realm and the Realm of Faerie?" Pip was a bit surprised. He grew up north of the wall but hadn't known its dual purpose. Not its magical one.

"It is a wall between Faerie and all realms," Merlin said. "There is little record of that time, but legend holds that the goblins were attacking the Roman legions, which is why they pushed them back. I'm afraid that when we broke the ordinarius from our realm into the Earth Realm, the barrier keeping Faerie separate from us was weakened, and all manner of beasts, both light and dark, might once again be free to roam our lands."

Dread dripped from Pip's mind into his chest and down into his belly. He didn't want to go north—especially not if there were dark *things* creeping out of Hadrian's Wall. Da had sat by the hearth on cold winter nights telling Pip, Mary, and his brother, Galen, stories he'd heard as a boy. Stories of beautiful elves who enchanted whole towns, of knobby wicked goblins with gnashing teeth who stole food from the poor, and of massive trolls as tall as trees who stomped around smashing villagers' roofs with their bulbous clubs. He shivered, clutching his fingers tightly into the triskele mark that had been left on his palm by the rune stone he'd sent with his sister. The elves didn't sound too bad, but he'd rather not meet a goblin or troll.

"We must go, lad," Merlin said, his voice gentle. "I need your knowledge of that part of the realm and may have need of your power to reseal the wall. You can help me assess the situation for the kingdom while you continue on your path as a battle mage."

"And what of Bowan?" Pip asked, hoping his battle mage mentor might come with them to ward off dark mages or goblins or trolls.

"Bowan will remain here in my stead." Merlin inclined his head toward the powerful battle mage. "If we are to unite the Kingdom of Britain, then we must seek to secure the stability of the south. And there is no better man to do it than Bowan."

Bowan grunted his ascent, and Pip wondered if he was glad of the job or resentful of it.

"And what shall I do, Master Merlin?" Alfred asked. Pip saw his aura swirling with hope and fear.

"You will, of course, come with us, Alfred. As our scribe and diplomat."

"Diplomat?" Alfred asked, his cheeks flushing pink. "I—"

"You speak as well as you write, in many languages, do you not?" Merlin asked.

"I—I do," the angel-faced scribe murmured.

Archimedes let out an indignant hoot as if to criticize Alfred.

"But of course I'm glad to come," Alfred said, glaring at the bird. "He's staying, isn't he?"

The bird rustled his feathers, turning his back on Alfred so he could look at Merlin.

"I'm sorry, my friend." Merlin spoke kindly to the bird. "You will, of course, stay here to aid Bowan should he need it."

Merlin turned to Alfred and Pip. "We must all use our gifts to assess the north and to stop the invaders from attacking while the south is secured. We will gather the remaining mages to our side if we can and put an end to the ways of the dark."

"What do you intend for me to do as a—a diplomat?" Alfred asked, and Pip heard the hint of the old Angel Face whine in his voice. The whine that said Alfred felt like he was powerless. "I shall, of course, write an account of what we discover and gather information for my maps. But as a diplomat . . ." he trailed off, for once at a loss for words.

Merlin leveled his gaze at the gangly scribe. If Alfred kept growing, he would soon be taller than Merlin. Except he was much thinner than the old mage. While Merlin had a jovial belly, Alfred resembled a willowy, angelic tree. All limbs, with a skinny trunk. "Yes, you shall write all we see and learn, you shall gather information for maps, and so much more. You, Alfred," he said, taking the boy's hands in his own, "you are to use both your skills as a scribe and a diplomat to aid in bringing gray mages to our side."

"Gray mages?" Pip had never heard the term before.

"Those who are neither dark nor light. Those who walk the path between our ways and the ways of Mordred," Caraline offered.

"You must help me sway Mordred's former soldiers and mages to the light, but I suspect many of their hearts have been too long obscured by the darkness."

"I'm to be a diplomat." Alfred sounded bemused and more than a little frightened.

"You *are* a diplomat, Alfred. Have you never noticed how well you speak in council? Your tongue sometimes spins golden thread from simple cotton." Merlin patted his arm reassuringly.

"He definitely knows how to talk." Pip snorted back a laugh. Alfred scowled, then smiled despite himself.

"You may think you have little power, but your power lies in your words. Those that flow from your lips and from your pen. That is where your magic lies. *We* will *all* do what is necessary to ensure the safety of our realm." Merlin gave a great sigh, then his aura seemed to burst with energy as he unfolded his plan. "Niall will come with us. He'll take a cohort of soldiers north to aid us on our journey. Bowan, you'll keep some soldiers here to hold the south and prepare a place for us in Winchester. Now, ready the soldiers."

Without comment, Bowan rose to heed the old wizard's command. A moment of panic jolted through Pip. Niall was a great magus-solider, but he was no battle mage. Arthur had always leaned on Bowan's command. Would Niall know what to do? Would Pip?

"Bowan," Pip called, stopping the battle mage at the threshold. "What are we to do with the dark battle mages who refuse to join us? They may fight." Pip's voice was harsh. He didn't want to be sent back to battle. He wasn't a warrior yet. He didn't even feel like a full mage.

Bowan turned, no trace of compassion in his battle-hardened face. "Many will fall. For those who survive, give them no choice but to comply." Bowan's eyes were steel. "And if they refuse, take prisoners and bring them back with you."

"Prisoners?" Alfred's voice squeaked. "Can you imagine *me* taking prisoners?"

Pip nearly laughed at the idea of Angel Face taking prisoners, but the thought of going on this journey—especially without Bowan—was too terrifying. Bowan had been there when Merlin first saved him and his mother and Mary from the slavers. He'd gone after Pip when he'd run away and been trapped by slavers. Bowan had saved Pip's life.

Merlin seemed to understand the fear in the room and addressed it quickly. "Bowan is our best defense against attackers. As I said, we need him to defend our hold on the south and help oversee the construction of the new garrison at Winchester."

"Niall understands how to command," Bowan said, and just for a moment, Pip thought he saw a crack in the battle mage's façade. A moment that said Bowan wished he could go with Pip. But the look was gone so quickly that Pip wondered if he'd seen it at all. "He'll continue your battle training. I expect you'll be a battle mage when I see you next."

Pip snorted. He was a mage, but he did not see himself as a battle mage.

"Go now, prepare your satchels," Merlin commanded his three apprentices. "Bowan, you and Niall prepare the men. We'll leave two days hence."

Well, if they all had to go, then Pip would protect Angel Face with his life. Alfred wasn't meant for battle, and neither was Caraline. Whatever his new role in this world was meant to be, he knew one thing: He would protect them both.

Three

Pip tossed restlessly on his straw pallet in the circular stone room that had become his own. This would be his last night here... his last night in his own bed. His last night in his new home.

Home. Maybe he wasn't meant to have a home; maybe he was meant to have a life of adventure and battle. When he came back south, *if* he came back south, Winchester would be where he would live. For that is where Merlin intended to move the heart of the new government, Aurelian Council of Mages and all.

Tiny bits of straw poked through his nightclothes, itching and tickling him more than usual. Pip grunted in frustration, tossing off the wool blanket that clung to his sticky legs. If only he could sleep!

After a few rough breaths, he laid back on his pallet and inhaled deeply, reminding himself to calm his mind the way Caraline had instructed him.

"Think of nothing. Let the darkness surround you. You are always safe in your visions," she would say.

He could almost smell her herbs of lavender and verbena. He breathed again even more deeply, and his eyelids grew heavy. Darkness enveloped him, wrapping its arms comfortingly around him. Yes, he was safe here, no matter what he saw. He took another deep, slow breath. Lavender, verbena, and—what's that? He inhaled again. The sea?

Pip found himself standing in the leather boots of a muscular, powerful man. It was as if he were the man himself. He knew his body and his mind. Wind whipped through his hair, unleashing blond strands from the braid that fell partway down his back and blowing blond wisps in front of his frigid blue eyes. His name was Halfdan Ragnarsson.

Pip's mind receded from the man, and he saw him as though a bird in flight, yet he was still within the man. He took in all that the man saw and felt and knew. Halfdan Ragnarsson stood on the prow of *Long Serpent*, a magnificent long ship with thirty oarsmen on each side and a massive white sail. It was a ship more masterfully crafted than any other he'd ever seen.

The season of raiding was Halfdan's favorite time of year. But this year was different. This year would be more than a raiding and pillaging. This year would be a time of conquering new lands.

Behind him, he heard the chants and laughter of the men and women aboard the twenty-six ships that followed in his wake. Nine times three. The numbers of the gods. Twenty-seven ships and more than five hundred dark warriors among the magic-tinged farmers. They were all prepared to lay siege to any resistance they encountered. And they were all loyal to him.

It was as if Halfdan had been summoned to this new land. A great change had occurred, a shift in the order of the world. Some of his people had vanished, and those with magic had been left wondering what curse of Odin had ripped their non-magical families from them. But Halfdan hadn't worried, he'd been ecstatic. The weak ones had been taken away, leaving only those with power. And from them, he had collected the strongest dark mages he could find for this invasion.

When his great priest, his clan's *gothi*, had told him of the foreign king Mordred's death, Halfdan knew it was time to seize the dead king's lands. A place where they could grow not only crops to feed his people, but also a place to embrace their ways without interference from other jarls.

Like a dam being broken, a river of magic had gushed forth, urging him toward the green coast. The *gothi* had called it Britannia and mentioned its northern wilderness as a place rife with dark magic.

Pip shifted uncomfortably within Halfdan's skin. Halfdan's cruelty, his darkness, threatened to overtake him, but Pip couldn't leave. Not yet. He needed to know what Halfdan desired.

The land grew from a speck before Halfdan's eyes into a verdant landscape ready for reaping. There would be gold and jewels, but also land where his mages could live and farm. He would build halls where his dark mages could study, and the followers of the fallen Mordred would join him.

Øvind, Halfdan's second-in-command, who bore a scraggly beard and thin scar from lip to nose, clomped over to Halfdan, who stood at the bow. "We'll make landfall soon."

They scanned the coast that rose before them.

"If the *gothi* is correct, we'll have no resistance. Perhaps a sacrifice will ensure our place among this land and will draw our gods to us." Halfdan's finger lingered briefly on a scar that ran along his forearm, a place he'd cut himself when a blood sacrifice, a *blót*, had been required. He would tell no one of his full intentions. Not Øvind, not the *gothi*, not his wife. They would learn in time, and they would obey him. He was meant to be more than a jarl. He was meant to be king.

"Go make preparations for landing," Halfdan told Øvind, who nodded and left to bark orders at the crew.

Seeming to know she'd crossed his thoughts, Halfdan's wife, Agata, appeared, a fur cloak hanging loosely down her back.

"I'll go with the raiding party." Agata stood beside him, her blond hair pulled back in braids.

"You will remain on the beach and make camp." Halfdan's words were clipped. Too often she argued with him in front of his men. Too often she wanted to fight.

"I will not." Her lip stuck out slightly, quivering in the way that used to make him smile at her strength. Strength that he now saw as defiance. Still, it was good she was such a powerful sorceress. He would use her blood in the ritual to raise the dark gods of this land and those of his own.

Halfdan turned her to face him, his hands resting on her shoulders.

"My love. I know you wish to explore . . ." She stiffened, her chin held high. "But I need you here to help prepare for the *blót*. We must make ourselves known to this land's dark gods. We must seek their aid to fulfill our desires."

Wild wisps of blond hair fluttered around her face as she appraised him. "You'll include me in the *blót*?" She'd always wanted to be part of the blood sacrifice, but the *gothi* had always refused her.

"I will. These are new lands with new laws. Laws I will create."

"But what of the *gothi*?" She frowned and rubbed a hand across her growing belly. Halfdan hoped it would be a boy. He needed a son to whom he could teach their warrior ways.

"The *gothi* has little power here." Halfdan sounded harsher than he'd intended. "He'll do as I command."

"But he is your brother."

Halfdan shrugged. "Yes. Gulla is my brother, and our *gothi*. And I am his jarl."

"And if he refuses?"

"Then he shall not take part in the *blót*. And only Odin will have the power to spare him for disobeying me."

"Then I agree." She stared deeply into Halfdan's eyes, her ferocity making Pip quiver. "I will stay at camp to protect our child and prepare for the ritual."

"Good." Halfdan kissed her forehead. "Then pray to Odin we encounter none of the foreigners until it is done."

"It will be as you say," she said, a fierce look of battle-longing flashing on her face before she kissed him. Honey and sea salt danced on his lips as she walked away, no doubt to prepare the chalice.

It would not be long until they reached the shore, and the sun fell and Halfdan would reach out to Loki, the father of monsters. With a good sacrifice, Loki would help him summon one from *Niflheim*. Halfdan would raise a powerful spirit from the world of mist and darkness. Perhaps even one of Loki's sons would come and visit them. Halfdan would raise a being more powerful than his people had ever known. Then everyone in this new land would have no choice but to obey him.

Pip's eyes flew open. The morning sun barely crept through the arrow slit window of his stone tower, but he was wide awake. That had not been a dream, but a vision. His power as a seer was growing, Caraline had been certain of that. And now so was he.

He tossed back his coverlet and rose with haste, no longer sorrowful that he must leave his room or his southern home. If what he'd seen was true, despite all they had done to protect their people, they were all in even more danger than when Mordred had ruled the land. Pip feared that with Mordred gone, this new darkness could threaten their entire realm. Bolstering the certainty of his gut was the taste of salt from the northern sea still fresh on his wind-chapped and bloody lips.

Prepared or not. Battle mage or not. Pip knew there was no choice except to go north.

Four

Pip settled in on the back of a cream-colored warhorse Bowan had gifted him before setting out on the journey. He knew going north was the right thing to do. They needed to assess the north and ensure any remaining dark mages were dealt with. So his short sword was sheathed within his saddle scabbard and at an easy reach. He hoped that by working on spells, learning to block his aura, and continuing to train on the road, he would be better able to help in battle. What good was a mage to an army if he couldn't hold his own in a fight? He sighed, praying that Alfred would be kept safe and hoping that whatever Merlin saw in him was justified and enough to help stop the onslaught of Northmen he'd seen.

He patted the horse affectionately. She was a sweet horse with a pale purple aura. Bowan had said that purple was rare for an animal and that a good horse could save your life in battle. Even Alfred had been given a horse as a parting gift from the great battle mage. Alfred's horse was a chestnut steed with soft ears, a friendly snort, and an aura to match his coat.

The dew-kissed landscape rose like the swells of a forgotten sea as they headed north. It was almost summer, but winter's nip was still in the air. Pip shifted uncomfortably in his saddle, wrapping his new cloak around himself to better block the biting wind. It had been months since he'd spent long hours on horseback. They'd only been gone from the castle at South Cadbury for a mere two days, and his legs felt like sticks that had been bent into uncomfortable new positions. But he knew his body would soon be used to the saddle again.

Alfred broke away from the line of about one hundred magi-soldiers and mages and rode up beside Pip, slowing his horse to a walk. "Aquae Sulis is just ahead. I wonder if Merlin and Niall will have us make camp? It'd be nice to have a meal other than hardtack." Alfred bit a piece of the hard bread-like biscuit and made a face. "It's better than nothing, but ugh, I don't know how soldiers can stand to eat this on long campaigns."

Pip ignored his own grumbling belly and scanned the hilly landscape behind them and the winding River Avon before them. Dark clouds spread across the sky like a fresh bruise. "Perhaps we'll sleep indoors tonight," Pip said, recalling a hillier landscape from when he'd travelled through Aquae Sulis with Pip and Alfred in the autumn on their way to King Arthur in South Cadbury. "Are you sure we're near Aquae Sulis? This doesn't look familiar."

"I'm sure," Alfred said with a nod. "I studied the maps closely before we left the fortress. There are hills all around us, but we decided on a less strenuous route through a valley to save the horses and the troops' strength."

Alfred was probably right. Pip hadn't studied the maps, and he'd never been this way. "We came in from the north before," he said, which is probably why he didn't recognize it. Still, he remembered Aquae Sulis and the fearful woman and the starving child he saw when he'd been here before. He'd given the boy bread, which he'd taken hungrily before his mother had ushered him into their small hovel. Pip had sensed no magic on them and wondered if their lives were better now in the Earth Realm. He hoped so.

They rode a short while longer, making their way toward the decrepit city of Aquae Sulis. Pip recalled the unkempt and crumbling stone buildings. No farm animals were about as there had been last time, and the waste that had been tossed on the street had been washed away by rain. He wondered if some of the farm animals had disappeared with the ordinarius or if they had been taken in by the magus left behind.

"It seems deserted," Pip whispered to Alfred, as if his voice would draw some dark creatures from the crumbling city walls. "It was lively last time. So many people and animals. And food in the city." His stomach rumbled in response.

Alfred laughed. "See, you're hungry, too. And not just for another bit of hardtack."

Merlin quickened his pace to ride beside the boys and then pointed toward the city, which rose before them in rambling stone and wooden structures. "Our scouts have told us Aquae Sulis is sparsely populated since the breaking of our worlds. Many of the people who lived here were ordinarius and went to the Earth Realm, and those who remain are weary and uncertain. Many are hiding out of fear of the dark mages who still roam. We will seek shelter at Caraline's old shop and the surrounding buildings not in use, and we will explore the city in the morning."

Pip watched Merlin ride toward the back of the line to speak with Caraline, and Pip hoped she wouldn't be too distressed at seeing her old home.

Despite the crumbling buildings, it was exciting to be back in a city. Alfred and Pip rode at the front of the line, anxious to see how many things had changed in the few months since they'd been there.

Single file, the troop of eighty magi-soldiers and a handful of battle mages rode into Aquae Sulis, the horses' hooves making clippity-clop sounds that echoed off the cobbles and the old stone walls.

Not long after turning onto the main road, Pip felt a prickling sensation on the back of his neck . . . as though someone or something was watching them. He glanced right, then left, but saw no one. Perhaps the eerie silence had him on edge. Or perhaps it was just the remaining residents watching them from in hiding.

As they rode into the city center, toward Caraline's old home, Pip thought he caught a glimpse of a man's wizened face peering at him from an upstairs window. Another time he saw a woman and her daughter hurry into a ramshackle house, a twist of smoke rising from its chimney. That must be what was causing the prickling sensation of being watched; he must be sensing the auras of frightened people.

A twist in the road took them onto a street crowded with buildings. Pip had forgotten how close together some shops and houses had been. Some were so close they seemed to twist together and blot out the sky. It wasn't long before they turned a corner and Pip recognized the well-worn wooden door of Caraline's herbalist shop and home. Pip craned his head to look for Caraline, but couldn't see her past the long line of soldiers between them.

Hoping the place hadn't been ransacked, Pip tied his horse to a post nearby and slowly approached Caraline's door. Other mages and soldiers did the same in front of other buildings along the street, knocking on doors to see if they could lodge within.

Pip reached for the latch on Caraline's door, then stopped. He had the same sense of someone following them. Something was watching him. He looked right. Then left. Then behind him. Nothing was there except his fellow magus tying up horses and knocking on doors. He shook off his uncertainty and turned back to the door. He reached out to see if he could open it.

"Shouldn't you knock first?"

Pip jumped and whipped out the dagger Niall had instructed him to keep in his boot, then huffed in relief. "Don't do that, Alfred!" Pip snapped, scowling at the angel-faced scribe who'd snuck up behind him.

"What?" Alfred asked, looking innocent.

"Don't sneak up behind people. Especially not soldiers or battle mages," Pip said and sheathed his dagger. "I don't want you to get hurt."

Now it was Alfred's turn to scowl. "You won't hurt me. You may have lost your way with weapons, but I believe you have more control than you think."

Without knocking, Pip shoved open the door with what sounded like a growl. "I haven't lost my way . . . I'm just—trying to find the right weapon."

Alfred held up his hands for peace and quietly followed Pip into the shop.

The same wooden table, stained with herbs and spices, where Pip had first met Caraline and enjoyed her fresh bread, was pushed toward one wall. A chipped pestle and mortar sat at the table's center. The fireplace, blackened with soot from years of use, was cold, and a few bundles of dried herbs still clung to pegs against the room's far wall. The room still smelled faintly of lavender and verbena.

A rustling noise and creaking sound from down the short hall stopped Pip where he stood.

"It—" Alfred began.

"Shhh," Pip hissed and held up a hand. "Listen."

The boys stood still, listening intently. No rustle. No creak. Just silence.

Pip shook away his uneasiness and stepped forward to touch the oak table where he'd once supped with Caraline and Merlin. He ran a finger along its edge and noticed the lack of dust. It appeared that Caraline had left quickly, but not so quickly that she'd abandoned the place without her belongings or care. Still, it seemed that some dust would have gathered in the months since she'd left.

"Look at this." Alfred's voice cracked against the silence. He bent down and dipped his fingers into a small ceramic saucer on the floor. "A dish with water in it. It looks as if someone's—"

Before Alfred could finish, they heard a swish, and both boys looked up to see the sleek black body of a young feline slither into the room. It watched them with uncertain curiosity before settling to groom itself in a ray of sunshine that sliced through the window with its warmth.

"A cat." Alfred grinned. "Now we know who the water's for."

"Yes." Pip frowned. "But who's been in here caring for it?" He hoped it was an old friend of Caraline's and not a dark mage. Not that a dark mage would care for anything other than himself.

The cat, who Pip now saw had a small tuft of white fur beneath its neck, sat bathing itself while keeping one green eye on them. It had a nice aura, emerald green like its eyes, and it was strong for an animal.

Alfred crouched down, attempting to coax the cat to him with a bit of hardtack from his pocket, when they heard Merlin and Caraline's voices float through the door.

"The city appears nearly abandoned," Caraline said, her voice tinged with sadness.

"Nearly, but not completely. Hopefully many of those who were on our side against Mordred are still here. If they are, we'll find them." Merlin sounded weary, but nodded encouragement as he led Caraline into her old shop and home.

As soon as Caraline saw the black cat, she let out a cry and rushed to stroke it.

Suddenly, the animal quivered, and its aura radiated outward. The fur on its back bristled, and before Pip could blink, the animal's arms and legs and torso extended, and the fur receded until standing before him was a girl who looked to be about his age. She was pale with jewel-green eyes and jet-black hair. Her face was sweet and shared something of the innocence of Pip's sister, Mary. Pip's heart stung.

She was dressed in a simple black frock that folded close to her body, and Caraline hugged the girl in a ferocious embrace.

"Oh, Gwenn. I'm so glad you're here. I sent word, but . . ." Caraline's words trailed off into tears, and the girl buried her face in Caraline's cloak.

After a very long hug and a few sniffs, Caraline wiped her eyes and the girl's, then turned toward them. "Merlin. Pip. Alfred. This is my niece, Gwenn." Caraline beamed.

"She's a . . . she's a . . ." Pip stammered as though his brains had been addled.

"She's a cat sìth!" said Alfred in perfect Scottish Gaelic, then proceeded to look her up and down as if she were some new species of frog he'd captured for examination. "Some ordinarius and magi, those up north where *he's* from," Alfred inclined his head toward Pip, "they say the cat sìth can steal a person's soul before it passes over to heaven. They won't light fires so they won't attract cats to the warmth, and they even use cat nip to distract them. Sometimes they even hold watches, called *Fèill Fhadalach*, to keep cat sìth from a corpse before burial."

The girl's cheeks blossomed in anger, and her aura deepened to a rich velvet green.

"*I* don't believe those things!" Alfred protested. He'd never been overly superstitious and, from what Pip had seen, had always tried to be kind. "Besides, it was mostly the ordinarius who told those tales, and they're not even here anymore."

Poor girl, Pip thought, remembering all too well being the subject of Alfred's scrutiny when they'd first met. He didn't like seeing this girl—Gwenn—look uncomfortable. Perhaps Merlin would intervene. He looked to his master, who simply appeared amused; Caraline, much less so.

Alfred was oblivious to them all, his entire focus on Gwenn. "Others believe that cat sìth will bless any house that leaves milk or cream out for them." He paced around Gwenn, continuing his study, then stopped, suddenly aware of himself. His eyes grew wide, and he looked sheepishly at Gwenn, his own cheeks reddening. "I promise, I don't believe any of that superstitious nonsense . . . it's just . . . it's just all so fascinating."

Alfred reached out to touch her, but Pip stepped between the girl and the scribe. *Dung head*, Pip thought. "Don't mind him." Pip smiled kindly at the girl. He had an urge to protect her like he wanted to protect Mary or even Alfred—when he wasn't acting like an idiot. "Alfred studied me when I first met him, too."

Alfred smiled his angelic, friendly smile, looking momentarily taken aback, as if realizing how he'd been examining Gwenn. "My apologies, miss. It's just . . . I've just never met a cat sìth before, merely read about them."

Gwenn's cheeks flushed even pinker before she retreated to Caraline's side.

Caraline put a comforting arm around her niece. "Yes, well, I'm sure Gwenn doesn't need to hear a recount of superstitions. In my view, Gwenn has been blessed. Cat sìth are rare. And she has a unique gift that may well help us all." Caraline beamed at her niece. "And I see you've mastered the spell so your clothing transforms with you."

"I have, but it's tricky," Gwenn said with a shy smile. "I still need to wear dark colors; otherwise my fur doesn't look right. Mother said I had a bright red patch on my fur when I tried it once while wearing a red cloak."

Merlin laughed so hard that his large, wobbly belly jiggled. His blue eyes twinkled, and he reached out to welcome the girl, who immediately seemed more at ease. "Greetings, young Gwenn. I've been looking forward to meeting you."

Before Gwenn could speak a greeting in return, Merlin's belly growled like a hungry wolf.

"I think we'd better feed Merlin before he turns into the beast within his belly," Caraline said, earning laughs from everyone.

With a flick of her wrist, Caraline ignited a fire in the stone hearth. In the time it took for Merlin to check in with Niall, for Pip and Alfred to unpack and feed and water their horses, and for Gwenn to dust off a few old plates, bowls, and wooden spoons, Caraline had put together a bubbling stew with meat they'd brought and a few root vegetables from her cellar that hadn't gone bad.

While the stew simmered, Caraline used a bundle of dried chamomile from a peg on the wall to make them each a cup of steaming tea. Pip took a sip, and it warmed him up inside and out, causing all the uneasiness he'd felt coming into the city to melt away like ice on a sunny day.

"We'll sleep here for the night," Merlin said, taking another sip of the steaming brew. "Niall said all the soldiers and mages have found housing, some with provisions they can use. The magus they have encountered are weary, but seem glad of our arrival." He leaned back in his chair with a groan. "I do miss Mistress Adella's cooking though."

So did Pip. He missed the red-faced temperamental cook, even if she did once threaten his backside with a spoon. Her meals were delicious.

"Perhaps we can find a mage skilled in the culinary arts willing to travel with us and cook for you if my stew isn't sufficient?" Caraline teased.

"No offense, Caraline. Your stew is magnificent. But I don't expect a powerful magus like you to cook when we're on the road. There is much to teach them," Merlin said, gesturing to Pip, Alfred, and Gwenn. "And I still plan to have you become a full mage and join the council."

"We'll see if the likes of Faelen will permit it," Caraline said.

Before Merlin could respond, his stomach let out another howl of hunger, and he grinned so that his beard quivered, then patted his gut. "I'll ensure they do! Now, let's eat. One can survive with hardtack, but we cannot truly live without regular hot meals. And who knows? Perhaps our fires and the aroma of stew will draw the dark mages out of hiding so we might turn their ways?"

"Spoken like a true man," Caraline said with a laugh.

"Now, tell us, young Gwenn. When did you arrive in Aquae Sulis, and what has been happening here?" Merlin gazed at her.

"I—" Her voice cracked as if from disuse, then she began again. "I arrived here a fortnight after Mother and Father disappeared. I sent word to Aunt Caraline through a messenger in our village . . ."

Caraline nodded. "I received it. That's when I wrote to you telling you to come here. 'Twas only a few days later that I sent another missive letting you know Merlin had summoned me to South Cadbury and to meet me there instead."

"I didn't receive the news about South Cadbury, so I came here. I knew you would come." She smiled at her aunt. "I wanted to come to you sooner, but I couldn't find anyone willing to leave Ratae with me. Many friends disappeared when the world broke." Gwenn sniffed but didn't cry.

"I'm so sorry, my sweet." Caraline placed a comforting hand over Gwenn's. "I know it's been hard."

Pip's heart ached for Gwenn at what she must have gone through. His heart had been broken, but at least he'd had Merlin and Alfred and Caraline. Gwenn had been alone. And he'd known what was going to happen. He'd known his family was going to be sent to the Earth Realm, where they would be free. And while all the ordinarius would barely have any memories of the Magic Realm, he hadn't really given thought to all the magus left behind who hadn't known it was coming. His heart twisted in knots at how painful it must have been for their ordinarius families to disappear without warning. He hoped that Arthur's final decree had reached the edges of the realm and beyond, so those whose families had disappeared at least had some explanation. That they knew their families were safe. That they were free.

"But," Gwenn continued, looking at Merlin, "I know you did what was needed. What was right. My parents will never be threatened by the likes of Mordred ever again." She took a deep, steadying breath. "And I am ready to help you and the realm, however I can."

"I've no doubt you will serve the kingdom well. But first, tell me how it is you came here and what has been happening in the city."

While Caraline and Alfred served them stew in which they softened their hardtack to be more like edible crackers, Gwenn spoke. And as she spoke, they ate.

"When I couldn't find anyone to travel with me, I used my power . . ." She looked to Caraline, seeking approval.

"Gwenn's parents didn't like her transforming on account of the superstitions. You did the right thing, Gwenn. I doubt there are many left who would blink if they knew what you are. Your family is safer now, but so are you," said Caraline.

Gwenn nodded, then continued. "So I transformed into a cat. I could hunt easier that way and didn't need to eat as much. And I could seek safety in the trees and see better at night. I avoided some bands of dark mages, but mostly the woods were quiet."

"How many dark mages did you see?" Pip asked, wondering how many had been killed and how many remained.

"A few groups of three and then a couple on their own. No more than twelve ... They seemed uncertain, lost."

"Which direction did they travel?" Merlin asked.

"They moved north as I came south. I think they went back toward Mordred's fortress, but I'm not sure. It's only a guess ... But there were other things, too." Gwenn's green eyes took on a haunted, distant look. "Sometimes I heard things at night. Strange things . . ."

"What kind of things?" Merlin asked.

She shook her head. "Strange. Unlike any animal I've ever heard." Gwenn shrugged. "But when I got close to Aquae Sulis, I didn't hear them anymore. And then I came here." She looked around the cozy room. "I remembered visiting you with Mother and Father two autumns past and found my way easily enough. . . . At first I stayed a cat, and a nice man, Mister Kitchener, began feeding me and giving me water. He shared fish he'd caught from the river or a bit of egg with me. He'd talk to me like I was human. And I was lonely. So lonely. But I couldn't speak with him, being a cat." She glanced at Alfred, a small blush flaring on her cheeks.

"But he knew what I am, somehow. He's a mage, after all. And one day, he told me it was okay. That I was safe, and I could transform into my true self, and he wouldn't tell anyone if I didn't want him to. So I did." Her voice held a tinge of confidence that hadn't been there before.

"And he has told no one. He's kept my secret and made sure I ate. Oh, Aunt Caraline, you must meet him. When I came and you weren't here, I didn't know what I would do. The door was unbarred, but nothing had been disturbed. And then, when Mister Kitchener was looking for ingredients, he came inside and saw me. That's when he started feeding me. I don't know what I would have done without him."

After a warm meal and many stories and laughs, Pip, Alfred, and Merlin unfurled their bedrolls and settled by the fireplace for the night. Caraline, who hadn't been able to travel to South Cadbury with her bed and linens, stayed in her old room with Gwenn.

In a short time, Pip heard Merlin's familiar snore. The one that made him wish he could learn a spell to block his ears.

Snnnrrrrkkkk. Snnnrrrrkkkk. Snnnrrrrrrrrrkkkkkkk. Merlin blew his beard out of his mouth, snorted, and licked his lips as Pip had seen him do before.

Pip sighed, but instead of being annoyed by the old mage's snoring, he smiled. Being in a warm room and having a meal with Merlin and Caraline and Alfred and Gwenn had felt almost like when he'd shared meals with his family. Almost. His heart stung, but he let it sting. He'd been numb for too long after mother's death, and he'd learned the best way to move through the pain of loss was to embrace it. So he let his heart ache for his dead mother, for his father and brother and sister who'd gone to the Earth Realm, and then he let in the joy of the people around him who cared for him. He was glad to be part of their lives and have them in his. He hoped they could bring the same comfort to Gwenn. So he let that joy seep deep inside, and he didn't feel quite so lonely anymore.

Five

It was a bright, sunny morning when they stepped out of Caraline's shop and met with Niall, who was lodging in an abandoned home nearby. The burly, friendly magus was dividing the soldiers into smaller groups to explore the city and find able-bodied magus willing to become soldiers or mages who might fight or represent Aquae Sulis on the Aurelian Council.

Pip wore his tunic over woolen trousers, belted with a large leather belt gifted to him by Merlin, and a short sword sheathed at his side. "Wear it to scare away thieves and to protect yourself if you come across a dark mage," Bowan had told him before he'd left South Cadbury. And Pip would honor his word. Especially since Alfred chose to walk around this unknown city unarmed.

Some of the battle mages and archers had set up practice ranges in an open field nearby; they were to stay and practice and to evaluate the skills of mages and magus alike. Part of Pip wished he could go with the archers to practice shooting. It had been too long since he'd tried to use his power with his skill in archery, but Bowan and Niall had seen his lack of skill with the sword, and that is what he'd been practicing most.

"Later, lad." Niall clapped Pip on the shoulder. "There'll be time for fun later. And I've promised Bowan to keep up your training. So meet me at the training field when you return. I'll be here working with our men and any new recruits."

Pip grinned, realizing he had missed being on the road with Niall and the soldiers. He'd missed the excitement of working with other battle mages and practicing in the open where he wasn't confined by castle walls. Out here he somehow felt freer.

"Yes, plenty of time for practice later with the sword, Pip. You, too, Alfred," Merlin said.

Alfred blanched, and Pip snorted back a laugh.

"You . . . you mean you want me to use a sword?" Alfred asked.

Niall barked out a chuckle. "At least enough to defend yourself, young scribe. You'll do fine. You and Gwenn, both."

Gwenn gave them a sly smile, but she didn't say a thing.

"Don't worry, lass. Caraline visited me this morning and told me your father trained you some with daggers and short swords," Niall said. "I'm sure we can find a good dagger for you to use. You, too, Alfred. We'll find something that's easy to conceal and good at close quarters if someone gets too near."

"Maybe Gwenn can teach you a few things," Pip teased Alfred, who'd never wanted anything to do with swords or knives or arrows.

Alfred shook his head, but didn't respond. Gwenn watched them silently, and Pip wondered what she was thinking. Most women didn't know how to fight. There were no female soldiers, let alone battle mages, but if Merlin was considering allowing women into the Order of Mages, perhaps he would allow them to fight, too. Pip wasn't sure what he thought about that. It was bad enough seeing a man with his arm lobbed off or his skull cracked open on the battlefield. He couldn't bring himself to image that happening to Gwenn. Still, he was glad she knew how to protect herself.

"It's time we meet this Mister Kitchener and the others Gwenn told us about last night," Merlin said. "Perhaps there is more order to this city than it appears."

Gwenn led the way with Caraline by her side, followed closely by Merlin and the boys. They turned right, then left, then right again, until she led them into a large, open square that lay mostly in ruins. The city had been in decline before, but now it was desolate. Pip saw only a few people scurry across the square as if they were mice rushing nervously about for food, fearful of a cat lying in wait.

When Pip stepped into the square, a sudden chill wrapped itself around him, and the air crackled with lightning. The sky grew dark, and an intense pressure began building.

"Seek cover! We're under attack!" Merlin bellowed.

Before Pip could move, a blast of power illuminated the square, knocking Alfred and Gwenn from their feet.

Caraline screamed, and using her outstretched hand, she put up a protective barrier around Gwenn and Alfred, whom she pulled into an open doorway.

A blast of purple light erupted from Merlin's rowan wood staff, and that was enough to snap Pip into action.

Pip drew his sword, let a ripple of power flow into the blade, and stepped beside his mentor. The grip was warm but not uncomfortable as the blade blazed with fire. Ready or not, he would defend his friends.

The ground rumbled beneath them, making Pip stumble. He crouched low to keep his footing, sword held at the ready.

"Stay there and keep them shielded," Merlin shouted to Caraline, who was several steps away.

Hand still outstretched, she kept the protective barrier around her and Alfred and Gwenn, who both lay by Caraline's feet, pale and unmoving.

"Will they be all right?" Pip cringed at the fright in his voice.

"They're in good hands. Now open yourself to the auras around us and focus. We must locate our attackers." Merlin scanned the perimeter.

Pip saw no auras, so he unfurled his senses, letting tendrils of his power extend beyond himself, seeking anything that felt unnatural.

"There." He pointed with the tip of his sword. "On the rooftop. I can't see it, but I can feel it. Something's there. Something dark."

Merlin turned his attention to the spot opposite the square from where Caraline tended to Alfred and Gwenn. Pip was relieved to see them both sitting upright—still pale, but alive.

"Prove yourself worthy of the darkness and destroy them in the name of Mordred!" a deep voice boomed over the square, making Pip grip his sword harder.

"It's a dark mage," Merlin whispered so only Pip could hear. "I sense there are a few other young magus with him. They may yet be swayed. Put a protection barrier around us, but be ready if I cannot convince them."

Pip immediately put up the barrier spell he knew. He wouldn't let Merlin down. "I'm ready."

With a nod, Merlin stepped forward, and his voice rang out clear. "Those of you who wish to live in a land of peace, who wish for a united kingdom, for a place where all magus and mages have opportunities to pursue their strengths and help one another, join us. We are of the light and seek a final end to Mordred's dark ways."

His words were met with silence. Then a boy, slightly younger than Pip, slowly emerged from the shadowed recesses of an adjacent building. He took a tentative step toward them, then another.

Pip could see his aura now—swirls of blue and gold, tinged with the gray of dark mages. He tensed, his grip tightening on the sword. The boy's aura was at odds with itself, and Pip wondered if the boy would fight or join them.

Merlin angled his staff toward the boy, not aggressively, but prepared. "State your intentions."

"I—" the boy stammered. He looked over his shoulder at the roofline behind him, then at Merlin. Then, in a rush, he spoke and ran toward them in the same instant. "I wish to join you if they let—"

Before the last word left his lips, and before he could reach Pip's protective barrier, a bolt of gray energy shot from the rooftop, striking the boy dead. Scorch marks veined his skin, and smoke rose from his hair. Pip's stomach turned as though he'd eaten rotten meat. He wanted to cry and scream. If only he'd extended the protective barrier. But he hadn't known if the boy had meant them harm. Pip let out a scream of anger, and his power surged into the blade, making it grow white with heat.

"Careful, Pip. It is a tragedy, but losses are to be expected." Merlin spoke calmly. Then he directed his voice toward the dark mage. "Are you so afraid of the light that you'll skulk in the shadows and kill children? Let them have a choice which path they choose, but do not choose for them!"

His words were met with a shower of sparks directed toward Caraline, Alfred, and Gwenn. They hissed when they collided with Caraline's barrier, but Pip could tell it was an untrained magus who had sent the blast. He wasn't sure if Caraline could hold off the dark mage himself.

"Merlin," he hissed. "We need to protect them."

"I fear you're right, lad," Merlin whispered back and began edging his way toward Caraline and the children, while never taking his eyes off the shadowed rooftop.

They were almost within reach of Caraline when a cry of several voices went up suddenly, and a handful of armed magus surged around them. Their auras were tainted with darkness, some more than others, but Pip knew he couldn't stop to reason with them. He had to protect his friends.

The group of dark magus surrounded them, and a man in a dark cloak with black runes, Mordred's colors, emerged from the smoke. "You cannot destroy us all, Merlin. There is a new power in the north, and we are gathering to join them. You will fail."

Another blast of dark power erupted from the rooftop across the square. Stone scraped against itself as part of an ancient Roman façade collapsed onto the square, just missing Pip's friends.

"Let no one escape!" the dark mage yelled. "Attack!"

Then everything seemed to happen at once. Caraline cried out as a stream of crackling gray light pierced her protective barrier, making her fall backward into the rubble. Gwenn let out a scream that became a yowl as she transformed into a black cat, the fur along her back raised in a ridge, her teeth bared as she hissed at the attacking mage. Merlin strode forward shooting bursts of purple and gold at the dark mages.

Pip focused his energy on his white-hot sword and swung at the dark magus stalking toward him. He struck, then parried, then struck again in a series of blows he'd practiced with Niall. He was dizzy with smoke, his mind clouded with the haze of magic and the screams of injured magus. Then he heard Alfred scream.

Pip sliced through the nearest magus, cauterizing the man's neck as he cut clean through. He turned toward his friends and blasted another man with fire before his sword even made contact. He was almost to

Alfred, who held a quill like a dagger toward a leering dark magus who was attempting to stab him.

Pip's power surged into his blade, and he charged the dark mage, but before he reached Alfred, his hands were on fire, and the blade was ablaze. He'd lost control of his power, and the fire had liquefied his blade. He dropped the sword in time not to be scorched by the molten metal.

"Alfred!" he cried, charging forward without a weapon.

Then Gwenn was there, a ball of black feline fury.

Her claws and teeth gnashed at the dark apprentice's face. She gouged his eye with her nails and severed his wrist with a ferocious bite. The young man screamed and sank to his knees, holding his bloodied eye, before Caraline hit him with a burst of energy that made him fall still. Everything went silent. Lifeless.

Pip fell to his knees beside his friends, tears streaming down his soot-covered face. He had tried to protect them, but he had failed.

Gwenn was back to her human form, shaken but unhurt. Alfred had a small gash on his arm from when he'd stood up to the dark apprentice, and Caraline had a knot on her head, but they were otherwise unharmed. They were covered in dust and soot.

Gwenn led the group past the rubble to another square and up to a welcoming ivy-covered arched doorway.

"Gwenn, what happened? Are you hurt?" A large, jovial-looking man with a bulging middle stepped out to welcome them.

"Mister Kitchener." Gwenn wrapped her arms around the large man who squeezed an arm around her shoulder in return. "We're okay, but we were attacked on our way here."

"Attacked?" He frowned. "By whom?"

"Dark mages and some magus who were intending to follow them."

"*Humf.*" Mister Kitchener scratched his shaggy beard. "Mister Tait just received a missive that dark mages had been spotted seeking apprentices on the way north. We've kept all the children inside today because of it."

"The dark mages are likely gone by now," said Caraline, "and most of the dark magus who attacked us are dead."

Mister Kitchener gazed past them protectively. "We've tried our best to make sure everyone we know steers clear of the dark ways. We shall help bury the bodies."

"Thank you, friend," Merlin said, grasping the big man's hand. "I, too, had hoped to save them."

"Come now, Gwenn." Mister Kitchener turned toward the archway and gestured them inside. "Let's show your friends inside, and you can properly introduce us all."

Cracked stone flooring and the faint smell of sulfur greeted Pip as they entered the old building.

"I'd heard stories of healing waters here," Mister Kitchener said, "yet we've found none that heal. A warm spring gushes up from beneath the ruins there." He gestured to a part of the building that seemed to have sunken in on itself. "We've used it to bathe, but it leaves an awful stench."

Merlin went to inspect the stinky water with Caraline, but a bubbling echo of children's laughter drew Pip's attention to a small group of young magus who sat facing a mage with colorful sparks dancing from one palm to another. The fire sparkled red, then purple, then orange, then blue, and the flames leapt back and forth between his hands.

"That's Mister Tait," Gwenn said. She led Pip and Alfred over to watch the man's demonstration. He had dark hair with a few strands of gray and a strong, stubbled jaw. He wore a red sash that marked him as a full mage. The only full mage Pip could see.

"This, children, is a small example of fire magic." He grinned at a girl about Mary's age who sat in front. Pip hadn't practiced enough with fire magic to use it properly with his sword—today had been evidence of that. At least no one had been killed like Mother had from his lack of control with the flaming arrow.

"Here, Anna. Open your hand. Reach out to the fire with your mind. Feel yourself warm without getting burned." He offered the girl a small blue flame from his palm.

Pip tensed, ready to toss his cloak onto the girl should the fire burn her. But Anna simply giggled as the blue flame rolled from Mister Tait's hand into hers.

"It's like a warm tickle," she said, sounding slightly amazed. She opened her hand wider, and the flame flared, then closed it, and the flame went out. "Oh, pigeon poo." The girl scowled, and everyone else laughed.

"Well done, Anna," said Mister Tait.

"But it went out," she complained.

"Yes, but you held it on your first try. That is a great accomplishment!" he said to all the students. "Now, I want each of you to find a partner. One of you will call the flame using the word *aodh*. You will then feel the flame alight in your hand. Once it does, try to pass it back and forth. Don't worry about the size or color for the moment. Just focus on conjuring the flame, containing it in your palm, and passing it back and forth to each other."

The students immediately broke into pairs.

Smiling, Mister Tait came over to speak with his visitors. "Welcome, Gwenn. I see you've brought some friends."

Gwenn introduced Pip and Alfred and her aunt and the great mage, Merlin, talking more than she had since meeting Pip and the others.

"Yes, I know of Merlin. You're one of the most powerful mages of the realm." Mister Tait extended his hand in greeting.

"Mister Tait is a mage-priest," Gwen told them. "He is both Christian and druid."

Alfred, who had been raised in a monastery, gaped. "How can you be both?"

"A Christian mother and druid father," said Mister Tait. "It's not so uncommon."

Alfred frowned for a moment, then seemed to find some solution in his mind. "Like you, Pip."

Pip squirmed uncomfortably as everyone looked at him. "Um. I suppose. My da was raised at a monastery, and Mother was Christian. But

Da's father was a druid priest." Pip squeezed his right hand tight around the triskele scar he'd received when he'd passed the rune stone to his sister as the world was torn apart. The rune had belonged to their grandfather, Esoric. "My grandfather was a druid priest with *draoidheachd*."

"What's in your hand?" Mister Tait asked, unable to keep the spark of curiosity from his voice.

Pip hadn't realized he'd raised his clenched fist in front of him and was surprised to see it glowing with golden light. He shook his head at first, not wanting to show his scar. But what did it matter? It wasn't like he ever had to hide his power again. He slowly unfurled his fist, revealing the tattoo-like scar in the shape of the triskele scorched into his palm. Usually black, it pulsed with white and golden light, as if beckoning him to draw upon its energy.

"You are a powerful mage, indeed, young Pip," said Mister Tait. "Earth. Sea. Sky. All of creation in your palm. And if I'm right, I believe you can wield fire magic?"

Pip squirmed uncomfortably under Mister Tait's friendly gaze. "I'm working on it," he mumbled.

"Well, you're still young, and with Merlin as your teacher, I expect we'll see great things from you," Mister Tait said, then smiled at Merlin. "What did you think of our warm springs?"

"Intriguing," said Merlin, whose beard dripped with the evidence of having drunk the foul-smelling liquid.

"I believe it may have some healing properties," said Caraline. "May I take some?"

"As you like," said Mister Tait. "I think the stuff tastes awful, but Mister Kitchener here enjoys using it in our stew."

"It adds flavor." He winked at Gwenn, who wrinkled her nose and laughed.

"I don't like it either, but you can't taste it in the stew." Gwenn grinned at Mister Kitchener.

"Well, I'd best be off to the kitchen to prepare the midday meal, but first I've got a local farmer bringing in some supplies in exchange for healing herbs I've prepared for him. Mister Tait will show you our home. I'll see you later." Mister Kitchener gave a friendly wave, then disappeared through an arched doorway into the kitchen.

Six

"Since you're all here, I must give you a proper welcome to our humble school." Mister Tait gestured to the open area before them where students practiced conjuring and exchanging colorful flames. "To my knowledge, it's the first school of its kind. All magus can be educated here. Within these walls, the children will learn to harness their powers and use their *draoidheachd* of fire, earth, water, and wind. Those boys who do not qualify as full mages will still be able to strengthen their skills and apply it to field or farm, city or battle."

"And what of the girls?" asked Merlin. "I see you're teaching them as well."

Mister Tait shifted uncomfortably. "Well, I didn't think it fair to let their magics lie fallow—especially since so many of the children have lost family members. They need to stay busy. So, yes, I'm training them as well. Perhaps a new king will find that the power of women magus are just as useful as men." He looked at Caraline, but didn't meet Merlin's eyes.

"It's a grand idea, and one I hope you will continue," said Caraline.

"I fully agree," said Merlin, laying a hand on Mister Tait's shoulder. "I'm hoping to see Caraline here as one of the first female mages. To waste one's talent or power because of their sex is a disgrace. One I hope we can put behind us."

Just then a little girl tugged at Mister Tait's arm, tears streaming down her face. A sweet-looking young woman scooped her up, gave her a hug, and took her to an area where younger children were playing and napping.

"I realize, Merlin, why you and King Arthur chose to break the realms. However, it has caused many unexpected hardships." Mister Tait watched the young woman for a moment as she distracted the child with a toy until the girl's tears turned to laughter. "Both children and parents were orphaned. So this is not just a school, but a place for the displaced children to live." He placed a hand on his heart as if he felt the pain of loss. "My sister, Sophia," he nodded toward the woman playing with the little girl, "she lost her husband and daughter to the Earth Realm, and she's chosen to stay here and help me build the school and to look after the young ones who've lost their parents."

Pip had never thought about it like that. When King Arthur had commanded him to help Merlin break the worlds, he never even considered all the families he would be separating. He'd been too focused on finding his own family. Too focused on defeating Mordred and setting everyone free. True, those in the Earth Realm had scarce memories of their loved ones here—Merlin had seen to it that the spell that broke the Magic Realm from the Earth Realm would mute the memories of the ordinarius—but for all the magus left behind ... He saw the room with fresh eyes. Behind the smiles and dancing flames, many faces still bore the heavy burden of loss.

"Yet had you not done what you did, our families would have been separated anyway," said Sophia, coming over to them now that the little girl had joined a small group of young children playing with marbles nearby. "They would have been sold to miserable fates. At least this way, we know they will never be enslaved again. Even if we miss them sorely."

Merlin clasped the young woman's hand in his own. "I'm sorry, my dear. I gave thought to easing all our memories of one another, but I did not think it wise. If we forget the history of what befell us, I fear we might have repeated the same mistake in some other manner . . . I only hope that those in the Earth Realm never find cause to sell one another again."

"Look, Mister Tait." A boy not much younger than Alfred and Pip came up to them, his face illuminated by the blue flame that danced in his palm. "I can make it jump and change color." The flame jumped from one palm to the other, then it turned from blue to purple to pink to orange. "And when I do this . . ." he gritted his teeth in concentration and the flame vanished, "it goes out."

Mister Tait clapped his hands and laughed. "That's wonderful, Henry. And what did you think to make it go out?"

"I thought of its opposing element. Water." Henry said it like it was the most sensible thing in the world.

"Well done. See if you can show some of the others what you've discovered, and I'll be with you soon," Master Tait said. Smiling, Henry coaxed the flame back to life and went to show any of the children willing to listen.

Pip was good at battle magic, but he'd never really considered working to control the elements by themselves. Of course, he knew how to put fire into arrows and into the sword, but that had ended in failure. His melted sword was evidence of that. Alfred could have died. Pip frowned. Maybe he needed to conjure fire alone. Maybe if he could control the element, then he could use it better in battle. There was still so much to learn. He'd talk to Merlin about it later.

"You should meet Lord Maynor. He was the mayor here before . . . before the changes. He has done his best to keep us safe. Sophia," Mister Tait said to his sister, "please teach the children the next lesson on herbs for healing, and I'll be back to assist." To his guests, Mister Tait said, "This way," and beckoned them to follow him through a squat, narrow stone doorway that led into an adjacent building.

Torches lined the darkened hallways, the flames licking the walls and shadows dancing across the stone. Pip reached out to the flames with his mind and felt them answer, his palm growing warm.

"Merlin," Pip said, falling back a step to walk with his master. "Why haven't we spoken of elemental magic? Of earth or water or wind or fire?"

"You already had great power when we met, and I knew you could use it to help defeat Mordred. We hadn't the time to start from the beginning. And your power is so strong with fire that you hardly need to draw from the others."

"And yet I'm struggling with battle now." Pip scowled. "I—I lost control today . . . and melted my sword. Alfred could have been killed. I'm afraid of what could happen next time."

"But he wasn't killed, Pip. And you helped me stave off a band of dark magus. Your control of fire is something to work on as we travel," Merlin said, then motioned for Alfred and Gwenn to walk with them. "All *draoidheachd*, all magic, stems from the elements in the world around us. Pip, as you likely realize, you are particularly adept at fire magic and in using that power for battle."

"What about me, then?" Alfred asked with a frown. "I'm not a mage, yet I am here because I'm a magus."

"Yes." Merlin nodded. "You lack the power of a full mage, but your skills are invaluable. Alfred, without realizing it, you draw your power from the earth—from those items you use most: ink and paper."

Alfred's lips parted in wonder. "Ink from berries and minerals, paper from trees, quills from fowl, all from the earth."

"And what of me?" Gwenn asked. She strode so quietly beside them that Pip had barely realized she was there.

"I need to work with you, Gwenn." Merlin stopped, his gaze penetrating. "Yet I think you may have some affinity for wind and earth. We shall find out together."

"Come along," Mister Tait called from a brightly lit doorway where he and Caraline waited for them.

They followed Mister Tait into the scriptorium, a stone chamber filled with several writing tables, shelves of scrolls, and leather-bound books. Massive windows let in streams of light, and scores of unlit candles sat on side tables for those who worked in the darkest hours of the night.

A pair of large, ornately carved wooden doors opened from the scriptorium onto a covered terrace. Magi-priests worked beneath the vaulted ceiling, using the space as an outdoor place to write. The weather was nice, and Pip didn't blame them for working outside. Some copied down holy words and illuminated biblical manuscripts, others translated scrolls from languages Pip could not decipher, and some copied spells into leather-bound grimoires.

Mister Tait approached a scribe who sat illustrating a book of herbs. He offered a plant specimen to the scribe and waved his hands as he spoke, imbedding the plant onto the page of the book.

"Thank you, Mister Tait," said the scribe. "I don't have that one." Now that the specimen was in place on the page, the man illustrated the herb with magicked ink, making the plant look vibrant and alive as if it were growing from the page itself.

"That's amazing," gasped Alfred.

"Now I'll write all I know about plant," the scribe told Alfred. "If you'd like, I can teach you how to do it."

"Yes, please!" said Alfred. To Pip and the others, he said, "Just come back and find me before you leave." And then he was lost to conversation about ink and paper and spells with his fellow scribe.

A stern-looking man quickly approached the group from where he'd been reading a manuscript near the open door to the scriptorium.

"Ah, Lord Maynor," Mister Tait said. "Meet Pip, Gwenn, Caraline, and the great mage of legend, Master Merlin." He nodded toward Alfred, who was now attempting to imbed the stem of a plant into a page. "And that's Alfred with Edgar."

Lord Maynor bowed to each, then took Caraline's hand. "Caraline, it is good to see you. I wondered where you had gone after the disturbance that took so many from our city." His eyes blazed at Merlin, but Merlin seemed immune to the anger.

"It is good to see you, Godric, but don't be angry with Merlin. He did what needed to be done to prevent the likes of Mordred from doing such evil ever again—"

"And yet we have lost nearly eighty percent of our population. Most of the magus have stayed, yet there is fear. Dark mages have come through our inns and taverns, plucking those they can lure with a promise of land in the north, but they seek to bend them toward their dark ways."

"Gwenn and her friends were attacked on the way here," Mister Tait said.

Lord Maynor let out a heavy sigh and shook his head. "I'm glad you're okay. And I'm thankful to have Mister Tait set up a school and home here. I'm certain it has quelled the flow of our good young people being tempted by dark ways."

"It's our hope to set up other schools like this one throughout the realm," said Merlin. "What Mister Tait has done is a model for us all."

"It is." Lord Maynor nodded, then gestured to those who worked and those who spoke in quiet, animated conversations around them. "I can care for the city and our people here, but they need to know they're safe. We need a king. Someone they can look to for guidance. Someone they are willing to fight for. They would fight for King Arthur, but he's gone. Now who do we have left to lead us?"

"Merlin has formed the Aurelian Council of Mages," said Caraline, "which is leading from South Cadbury, and they are creating a new capital in Winchester."

"That's good, but what of a king?" Lord Maynor folded his arms in expectation.

"You know the prophecy," Caraline told him.

Pip winced. Not another prophecy. He'd already fulfilled the one about helping King Arthur defeat Mordred. Hopefully, this one had nothing to do with him. Alfred squirmed beside him, and Pip had a feeling that Angel Face had been keeping something from him.

"What prophecy?" Pip asked.

"*A warrior mage from the north foretold. Bearing scepter, triskele, steel, and flame, against his will, he will reign. A new kingdom joined, north and south. With power and justice he will see, all his people shall be free.*" Lord Maynor almost chanted the words, so they sounded holy. It was as though he'd spoken them a hundred times before.

Pip's stomach somersaulted in fright, but Alfred spoke before Pip's thoughts became clear. "And yet prophecy can be fraught with mystery. We don't know when such a king will emerge—it could be centuries from now." Alfred spoke quickly, filling Pip with relief. "It's why we haven't told you before, Pip."

Pip was glad they hadn't. True, he was a mage, he had the mark of the triskele, and he was from the north, but he wasn't a warrior or a battle mage. He melted swords! He couldn't even find the right weapon, so becoming a battle mage was nearly impossible. And the last thing he could ever be was king. He sighed again, thankful he didn't fit the prophecy.

"Or," said Merlin, "he could already be in our midst. Regardless, I expect we will find a suitable king to rule the south and keep back any invaders from the north soon enough. In the meantime, the newly formed Aurelian Council along with the remaining city leaders will ensure stability."

A young scribe who looked similar to Alfred, yet wore the robes of a magus-priest, hurriedly brought a scroll to Lord Maynor. "A missive, sir. Just in from those remaining at the northern edge of town."

Lord Maynor unfurled the scroll and skimmed the document, his brows drawing into a tight, dark line. "It is fortuitous you arrived when you have. Another dark mage has just departed Aquae Sulis. Likely the one who attacked you. He is taking a small group of powerful young magus north to train with some Northmen who have landed on our northeastern shores."

Merlin exchanged a worried glance with Caraline. "Now we have our confirmation. The Northmen have arrived."

Seven

Pip and Merlin set off with a young tracker called Cuthbert and a small group of magi-soldiers from Aquae Sulis. Merlin had left Caraline, Alfred, and Gwenn in Aquae Sulis with Niall. Alfred was to record how Mister Tait had set up the school and to devise a way for them to record all student names and records. Niall and the men would continue seeking magi who wished to join them, while recording all the names and ages of those who remained in Aquae Sulis. Caraline and Gwenn planned to tend to any sick or wounded and share their knowledge of herbal remedies with Mister Kitchener.

As the small group rode through an open field on the outskirts of the city, a raven cawed and launched itself from the crumbling city wall. Since Pip had become mage, the birds had been his friends, and yet since he'd left South Cadbury, they'd been scarce. This one didn't even come near, but merely circled overhead as if searching for prey. Pip felt the uneasiness creep over him again. The feeling that something was watching them.

After less than a day of traveling by horse, Cuthbert had them make camp. The obvious signs of the fleeing mage and his dark apprentices had disappeared, and Cuthbert had ridden ahead to scout and ensure they weren't heading into a trap. The gooseflesh on Pip's neck and arms had settled since leaving Aquae Sulis. Still, he felt as though something was following them. He couldn't shake the feeling, and he thought about telling Merlin, but what was there to tell, really, without more details?

"You worked with water when we first met," Merlin said, sitting down on a fallen log to rest while they awaited Cuthbert's return. "And you've used fire extensively in battle."

"Yes, and I likely killed my mother because of it," Pip said, remembering how his flaming arrow had ignited the tent his wounded mother had been trapped in.

Merlin let out a deep sigh. "You no more killed your mother than I did. Yes, you caught her tent on fire, but even if you hadn't, she would have succumbed to her injuries. You saw that, lad."

"But what of the blade in the square? I melted it! It seems I have as much control over fire as an animal does the fleas on its back." Pip scowled and kicked a pebble, sending it skittering across the ground.

"Then you must practice. Practice until it flows from you. Then you will be free to use fire, to use all the elements, all of your *draoidheachd* without thought. When that happens, you will become be the mage you are meant to be."

Pip sighed, then opened himself to embrace the tingle of power he felt coursing through his palms. Merlin was right. He needed to practice. He'd been so busy learning to become better with the sword itself that he had neglected to work on using fire.

After watching Pip play with fire for a few moments, Merlin continued his lesson. "Aside from water and fire, you also transfigured those men into squirrel-like beasts, which combines earth magic with pure *draoidheachd*."

"What do you mean, pure *draoidheachd*?" Pip asked, the sizzle of power flaring in his palm. He imagined a tongue of fire dancing on his hand like he'd seen at Mister Tait's school, and a purple flame sprang to life in his hand. The flame twirled around his triskele scar, glittering and changing color when he willed it to do so.

Merlin snorted back a laugh. "And you ask why I didn't start with elemental magic. You've not even had basic instruction in it, yet you can do what Mister Tait was teaching with no instruction at all." He shook his head so his white beard fluttered in the wind. "You are truly gifted, Pip, as you already know by the power you drew upon when you helped me break our realms. That is the power of pure *draoidheachd*. It is pure and raw and untamed. It comes neither from the earth or fire, nor from the water or sky. It comes from between the elements. From within and without. It is drawn from the very ether, and few mage can access it directly. And that, dear Pip, is what you must work on."

"Accessing pure *draoidheachd*?" Pip asked, making the flame flicker from purple to orange to blue to green as he tossed it from hand to hand.

Merlin nodded. "That, and control. And when you do, I believe you will discover your true power." Merlin's words drifted into silence, and he gazed into the distance for a long time as if seeing something Pip could not.

"I'll work on it," Pip said, already imagining a ball of water forming in his hand. In his mind's eye, he could see the dew from the grass snaking toward him, coalescing into a watery ball, which he held for a moment, then let seep between his fingers and back into the earth.

"Good," said Merlin. "Move through each of the elements, and then try to feel the space around you—the space between everything else. See if you can access the *draoidheachd* there."

Pip moved from water to wind, but as he did, the same uneasy feeling spread over his back and shoulders as if someone or something was watching them, and the small whip of wind he had conjured around them snuffed out. He looked to where Merlin gazed, but saw nothing. He glanced behind them and into the trees, but still nothing. That *nothing* was very wrong. He could always see auras, but he saw no aura of bird or beast or the men in camp. Perhaps it was simply his mind playing tricks on him. He shook off the shiver, hoping this feeling of foreboding was nothing more than his imagination and his concern over the dark invaders he had seen.

Then he heard something like the pitter-patter of rain in the distance—yet there was no cloud in the sky, only the glowing yellow, orange, and purple hues of the setting sun. The thudding beat grew steadily stronger. Placing his hand on the hilt of the new sword Niall had given him to replace the one he'd melted, Pip rose to his feet, and the men at camp snapped to attention.

Merlin placed a hand on Pip's arm. "No need to draw your sword, lad. It is only Cuthbert."

"How can you tell?" Pip squinted, trying to see movement or an aura through the mass of trees that gave off their own pale hue of living green. Then he saw a disturbance in the distance, a faint orangish-yellow glow bobbing slightly above a brown one. Cuthbert and his mount. "I see him now. His horse, too."

"Yes. Cuthbert is excellent at cloaking his aura when scouting and tracking, but he does tend to be a beacon when he's riding back with information. It's something *he* must work on." Merlin patted Pip's arm, then creaked to his feet. "Now, let's go see what news Cuthbert has discovered."

Sweat dripped from Cuthbert's brow as he rode to the small clearing where they camped, then dismounted from his horse and walked over to Merlin and Pip.

"There is a small settlement just over the ridge, at the meeting point of the five valleys formed by the River Frome. I see dark auras mingled with light. I believe that's where the dark mage and magus from Aquae Sulis have joined with others. There is still some light among them. Perhaps it's not too late to persuade some of them to join us."

"How many?" Merlin asked.

"About one hundred, as near as I could tell. Mostly men and boys, a few families and women. Perhaps the dark ones have offered them food and drink, and they are uncertain of where to go?"

"Perhaps," Merlin said. "Pip, what do you think? What questions would you ask?"

"Um . . . I'd ask how many are mages and how many are not. And what of their weapons and their horses? Are they all armed, or only some? If they are at the meeting point of a valley with women and children, then it seems like they are not preparing for an attack." He wasn't sure why Merlin wanted his opinion on the matter.

"All good thoughts and questions." Merlin swung his gaze back to their scout. "And do you have answers?"

"From what I could tell, most were not shielding their auras. About twenty were caring for their swords, and there is one blacksmith in the camp. A few children played around the fire. The darkest auras seemed to be concentrated at the camp's center."

"And how far ahead of us are they?" Merlin asked, his fingers tapping at the head of his rowan wood staff, which had the face of an owl carved at its top.

"About three miles to the north."

"Then we will stay out of sight. We'll camp here for the night, but light no fires. We should not approach them until all our men have joined us from Aquae Sulis."

The freshly baked bread of breakfast seemed a distant memory as Pip cleaned the hardtack from his teeth with his tongue. Without stew or soup to soften it, eating hardtack was almost like chewing salty tree bark. Not that Pip had tried tree bark, but it certainly seemed like what wood might taste like. He crinkled his nose, then flopped on his side, trying to find a comfortable position between the two large trees roots that made up his bed.

Since it was a brief journey and the weather mild, they'd brought no tents, just bedrolls. Still, he hadn't expected not to have a fire. He shivered and pulled his woolen cloak around him more tightly.

The day of riding had been hard, and despite being hungry, Pip was exhausted. So he nestled his head on a bed of dry moss and quickly drifted off to sleep.

Pip's eyes opened to the flames of a massive fire. Harsh voices chanted in the night, speaking words and names he didn't know yet somehow understood. He looked down, and again he was in the body of a large, muscular man. A man filled with pride and ambition. He was Halfdan Ragnarsson.

All around him, wild men and women chanted and danced around the flames. Many had painted faces, their hair in twists and braids. All wore knives, swords, and axes. They held cups to their lips and drank deeply. The fire flared high, shooting embers into the night sky, sending shadowy tendrils out over the revelers. The air crackled with excitement, and Halfdan grew impatient for something important he was about to do. Pip knew his feelings, but not all of his thoughts or plans. It was as if he were peeking into the strange world of this Northman.

"Bring him." Halfdan's deep voice boomed over the throng, who settled at his words.

Halfdan, a powerful battle mage and jarl, strode around the great fire to a place where two massive wooden posts jutted from the ground.

Two rugged warriors with designs of serpents and wolves inked on their faces led a man in a white tunic to stand before their jarl.

"Halfdan." The man in white spat the jarl's name, his voice heavy with spite but spoken only loud enough for Halfdan to hear. "Brother, why do you bring me out such as this? I did not approve this *blót*."

"I knew you wouldn't, Gulla, which is why I did not consult you— *brother*." Halfdan motioned for the two men beside Gulla to let them speak privately.

"Why do you scheme of summoning a dark one?" Gulla asked. "Why not follow Odin and love all our gods? Pray to Odin and Thor and Freyja and Loki."

"I do, brother, I do. And they have shown me that my path to power is through darkness. And this sacrifice will be just the beginning." Before Gulla could speak another syllable, Halfdan put his hands on Gulla's shoulders in an embrace, but Pip knew there was no love in it. "Gulla, my brother. Our *gothi*." Halfdan spun his brother to face the crowd and spoke loud enough for all to hear. "To help us, call upon Loki. . . . To help us bring our gods to be here with us, we must give sacrifice. And Gulla, our *gothi*, has offered himself for the *blót*, our first blood sacrifice in these new lands."

Gulla strained in Halfdan's grasp, but didn't speak. Halfdan felt a sense of grim satisfaction that he would sacrifice a priest to their gods. What better sacrifice could he offer? And, Gulla. Oh, Gulla. The dutiful, gods-loving son. He had prayed and worshiped while Halfdan had fought. It was the way of things for them. Always the way of things.

Gulla had not agreed to be sacrificed, but now that Halfdan had announced it, Gulla would not refute him. If he did, he would lose face with all the people who had followed his guidance for so many years.

Gulla would lose face with the gods themselves. No. He would allow himself to be sacrificed so he would not lose favor, and that was good. A willing sacrifice was more acceptable to the gods than an unwilling one.

Halfdan wished he could laugh at his cleverness. Disposing of the one person standing between him and the ritual would bring him closer to the gods than ever before, while also pleasing the gods with his *gothi's* death. It was perfect.

Horror roiled in Pip's gut as he realized Halfdan meant to kill his own brother in a sacrifice to their heathen gods, yet Pip was powerless within Halfdan, a mere observer of these strange, violent Northmen and their barbaric ways.

Halfdan barked out an order, and the two men who had appeared with Gulla led him to the wooden posts where they tied his wrists with ropes.

In their excitement, the people began chanting again in their strange tongue, and Pip grew slightly dizzy, as if he were being drawn into their ritual by some power he had never felt before.

A robed figure emerged from the crowd and presented a sleek steel blade on a bed of crimson silk. Halfdan turned his back to Gulla and faced the man presenting the blade.

Slowly, Halfdan slid his fingers along the length of the long knife from tip to base, its sharpness grazing his skin. He grasped the bone handle and raised the blade into the air. The people cheered, then continued chanting. His people.

"With this sacrifice, I call to Loki and his daughter, Hel. I call to the spirits of *Niflheim*." Halfdan turned to his brother, the people's chanting growing louder and more powerful. Unexpected tears crept into Halfdan's eyes, but his ambition quickly swallowed his grief. "Let this sacrifice of my brother, my own blood, and our *gothi* bring favor upon us in this new land. Let us plant and reap. Let us fight and win. Let us live and rule." Halfdan placed the edge of the blade against Gulla's throat, and their eyes met.

Gulla didn't cry or plead or beg for his life, but held himself tall. "I will feast tonight in Valhalla," he called so his voice reached into the heavens, and Pip wondered if his own God could hear the man. Then right before Halfdan drew the blade across his throat, Gulla whispered to his brother, "And may the gods give you all that you deserve."

Heart pounding, Pip woke with a gasp, his hand immediately at his throat where he'd seen Halfdan's blade slice Gulla's flesh. His hand was dry. No blood. No pain. Still, his heart thrashed, and he tossed aside his cloak, kicking it away from where it tangled in his legs.

Pip sat up and looked around the camp. The camp was silent save for snoring. The sky was dark, the moon peeking through the passing clouds. Most of the soldiers slept. Merlin slept. Pip could hear his snoring loudest of all.

Snnnrrrrkkkk. Snnnrrrrkkkk. Snnnrrrrrrrrrkkkkkkk. Merlin's familiar notes of sleep rang though the camp.

Pip sighed. He trembled at all he'd just seen of the Northmen's savagery, but slowly his heart settled. He saw no movement except for the two soldiers on watch who patrolled nearby.

Then Pip felt the prickly, tingly sensation again on the back of his neck. The same one he'd felt when he thought they were being watched. He scanned the darkness, listening to the gentle rustle of branches in the wind and the soft thud of the soldiers' feet against the moist earth.

Snnnrrrrkkkk. Snnnrrrrkkkk. Snnnrrrrrrrrrkkkkkkk.

He scanned the surroundings, seeking any strange auras. The soldiers' auras were dull in sleep, pale oranges and greens and browns and blues. The trees' and horses' auras even seemed more subdued at night. He saw nothing out of place, unless it was a spy with his aura tamped down. But surely the guards would have spotted it. Pip rubbed the sleep from his eyes and looked again. Nothing. He shook his head at himself. With all he'd just witnessed of the wild Northmen, his imagination was getting the better of him. No one was watching them.

Pip lay back against his mossy bed. Thunder rumbled overhead, and the splat of a single raindrop slapped against his cheek. He could still see the moon through the building clouds, and he prayed the rain would hold until they were safely back in Aquae Sulis.

Then a shadow caught his eye—something low to the ground, near the underbrush only a stone's throw away. Perhaps it was a hare or raccoon, yet it seemed larger. He could scarcely tell in the dark.

A flash of lightning revealed the shadowy outline of a creature with two legs and hunched shoulders. It had no visible aura, and its back was to him. But what was it? An animal would have an aura, but this thing was oddly empty of visible energy. Was this the being that had been watching them? Following them? Pip had been looking at human height and up into the trees, but not into the brush.

Pip rose from his bedroll, drew a dagger from a sheath at his ankle, and crept slowly toward the creature. He watched its movements. It paced when the soldiers paced, stopped when they stopped.

When another crash of thunder boomed and lightning flared, the strange being turned its head and looked directly at Pip. Its eyes gleamed marble-black, its skin a pasty green, and its snarling teeth were yellowing, needle-like spikes that looked as though they could tear the flesh from his bones.

Pip screamed. And in another flash of lightning, the creature was upon him.

Eight

Merlin was on his feet, his aura blazing white and purple. "*Prohibere!*" he bellowed. Light shot from the tip of his staff and suspended the creature in midair.

Pip scrambled backward, then circled around to stand behind his master.

"Secure the perimeter," Cuthbert barked, his hair poking in odd angles from sleep. "Ensure there are no other spies about."

The entire camp was awake now, and the magi-soldiers leapt to obey Cuthbert's command. All had slept in their clothing, swords at the ready. Still, Pip wished Niall was with them.

"What—what is it?" Pip stammered, peeking around Merlin to stare at the pasty, green-skinned monster, his heart hammering against his ribs even harder than when he'd witnessed Halfdan's sacrifice.

"I'm not certain." Merlin stepped forward to inspect the creature, who was still dangling mid-leap. Merlin circled it slowly, carefully studying it.

The thing made a gravelly gurgling sound. Merlin stepped even closer, tilting his head to listen. "What's that you say?" the great mage asked, inspecting an intricate mark on the creature's wrist.

Again the beast made the gravelly sound in its throat, and Pip realized it was speaking.

"Very well," Merlin said, as if he understood it with great clarity. "But if you attempt to run, if you attempt to harm this boy or anyone in this camp, I will restrain you. Do you understand?"

The creature made more gravelly noise and nodded, causing its large ears to flap at the tips like bat wings.

"Pip, do you have any hardtack left?" Merlin asked as he slowly lowered the beast to the ground. The power that had encased it disappeared.

"You're—you're letting it go?" Pip asked, staring in fear. "It could be a spy for the dark mages. Or the Northmen." The creature turned to look at Pip with large, suspicious eyes. "Why would you let it go?"

"He's no spy—merely hungry, lad. He said he originally followed some of the 'dark ones,' as he calls them. He's been living on scraps of food they leave behind. Apparently he scavenged some on the outskirts of Aquae Sulis, but he felt too exposed there. He followed us into the forest. Tonight he couldn't bare his hunger any longer, and he swears he can smell food on you." Merlin's gaze swung from the creature to Pip, but Merlin didn't lower his staff, which was still directed at the imp. Pip knew Merlin would strike if the beast attempted to attack again. "The hardtack, if you please."

"Uh, right." Pip ran his hands over his pockets until he found the piece of hardtack he hadn't been able to finish at supper.

"Go on. Give it to him." Merlin kept his eyes trained on the creature, staff at the ready.

Pip took a tentative step toward the beast, who growled at him. *Of course, you had to sleep with food in your pockets. You're lucky a squirrel didn't sneak up on you, too.* Pip grimaced, but stepped closer and then tossed the piece of hardtack to land at the creature's feet.

"What is it?" Pip asked Merlin.

The strange animal scooped up the hardtack in a swift motion with its pasty green hand and stuffed the entire biscuit in its mouth. It chewed ravenously, then coughed, spewing powdery crumbs several feet in front of it.

Pip flinched, but felt sort of bad for the beast. Hardtack wasn't very good, and it *was* dry. He didn't like the looks of this gnarly little monster, but Pip understood what hunger felt like. And he understood thirst. So, despite the nervous worms writhing in his stomach, Pip took the drinking skin from his side and tossed it to the creature, who caught it in its yellowing nails. It opened the skin and drank deeply, its beady eyes never leaving Pip.

"I believe," Merlin said after some thought, "that *he* is a hobgoblin trusted by the royalty of Faerie. Do you see the mark on his wrist? It's a sign of loyalty. I've seen it in ancient texts, but have never seen one. He should be safe—even helpful—to our cause, as the ancient texts describe the Fae being glad to have our worlds separated and not conjoined."

"A goblin?"

"A hobgoblin," Merlin said. "There is an important difference between goblins and hobgoblins. Goblins can be vicious creatures who dwell in dark magic. Hobgoblins, while sometimes mischievous, prefer creatures of light. This creature speaks a form of Faerie, the common tongue of their realm. I studied the language many years ago. Alfred will need to learn it now, too. I'm sure he'll find it fascinating."

"And what . . ." Pip stuttered. "What is he doing here?"

The hobgoblin wiped his mouth on a tattered woolen sleeve and made more gravelly noise, from which Pip could begin to discern some pattern of language.

"He says his name is Ælfstan and that he was a guardian of the wall," Merlin translated for Pip. Then, in the same gravelly language, Merlin spoke to Ælfstan.

"He's traveled a long way. All the way from Hadrian's Wall," Merlin said finally. "The Romans were clever. As I was telling you before we left South Cadbury, when they built the wall to hold back the unruly Picts to the north, the Roman mages used their power to push back the beings of Faerie as well. The land there is rife with magic, and the creatures from Faerie were causing mischief along with the barbarians who fought the Romans."

Ælfstan spoke again, and Merlin nodded. He lowered his staff and led the hobgoblin to a small clearing, mumbled a few words, and started a fire with his hands. It was a small fire with green flames that issued no smoke, only warmth. Ælfstan quickly huddled in front of it, warming his bony fingers.

Pip's heart twisted for the hobgoblin. He was ugly and frightening, but perhaps Pip had judged him too harshly. He was still one of God's creatures—perhaps—and he was cold and hungry and far from home. Pip knew what it felt like to be all those things. So Pip went to his pack and pulled out a small fur hide he'd brought along in case the nights grew cold. Ælfstan needed it more than he did, but he wasn't certain of how to present the pelt to the hobgoblin.

Pip crouched near the fire at arm's length, studying the creature while he spoke to Merlin. The hobgoblin had tall ears that pointed at the tip, almost like the elves Da had described, except not beautiful or fair. Hair sprouted from Ælfstan's ears like dandelion puffs, and he sniffed the air with his large, bulbous nose.

The hobgoblin stopped mid-conversation and twisted to look at Pip. He made a strange guttural sound and was suddenly beside the boy. He'd crossed the short distance so fast Pip had barely seen him move.

Pip scooted back in alarm, but Merlin just laughed.

"He asked why you're staring at him," Merlin said, then warmed his hands as if it were nothing to sit conversing with a hobgoblin.

"Um ..." Pip hadn't meant to stare, but he'd never seen a hobgoblin before.

"A moment ... if I can remember," Merlin said, and his eyes shifted in thought. After a long pause, he pointed his staff at Pip.

A glowing warmth spread through Pip from his heart to his head.

"There." Merlin set his staff into the ground with a satisfied thud. "I've cast a spell on you, Pip. It shan't last more than a day, but you should be able to understand our guest now, and he, you. I think it's important that you can speak with him. He has much to tell us of the north."

Pip swallowed the egg-size lump in his throat.

"Have you never seen a hobgoblin before, little mage?" The hobgoblin's voice was still gravelly, but Pip now understood his words.

"Um," Pip began. "Uh, no. I—I thought hobgoblins were only in tales told to frighten children from going into the woods alone at night."

At that, Ælfstan laughed a guttural, hearty laugh. "It is wise to be cautious in forests at night, with or without hobgoblins."

The hobgoblin shivered, and Pip, realizing he still held the animal pelt, offered it to Ælfstan. "Here. This is for you," Pip said, handing the hobgoblin the fur. "A gift to help you keep warm."

The hobgoblin took the pelt, fingering it gently before placing it around his bony shoulders, all the while, watching Pip. "He shall be a great mage one day," Ælfstan said to Merlin. "Perhaps the greatest of the realm. And yet . . ." his dark eyes danced in the eerie firelight, "he is young, even for your kind. And there is much that could keep him from growing into the mage he is meant to be. There is much to fear."

"Tell us, please, what you know of the north," Merlin said. "What happened that brought you to our world? And what of the dark mages and their plans can you share?"

"You ask many difficult questions, and I am a mere guardian of Faerie. But I will answer as best I can." Ælfstan snugged the fur pelt around his shoulders and let out a sigh, then he spoke again. "There was a great disturbance in the *draoidheachd*. I was guarding the Great Wall, as we call it, ensuring no humans entered our realm, and there was a rippling in the veil between our worlds. An eddy appeared in the stone, and when I approached to discover the cause, I was pulled through. It was as if I had fallen headlong into a great whirlpool. Yet the stone was not hard, but cold and confusing. When I awoke, I was in your realm.

"I searched the wall for days seeking a way back to Faerie, but could find none. So, cold and hungry, I have been wandering the forests and outskirts of your human towns ever since." Ælfstan rubbed his hands together, appearing deep in thought. "Being here, I have heard and understood snippets of the conversations of men. I have learned that when the dark one, Mordred, was killed, there was a ripple in the veil— for he had used his power to help enhance the wall to keep our worlds apart. And when he died, there was a weakening. Some of his power went with him, and the wall trembled."

"Yet the wall still holds?" Merlin asked, concern etched in the deep lines of his face.

"From what I saw, it does . . . for now. But I and my Faerie kin sense a great darkness coming upon the land. One even darker than Mordred.

One in which we do not wish to partake. Pains will be taken to enforce the magic of the wall on our side, but your side is weak. And it must be reinforced lest more of my kind are pulled through."

"And what would happen if they are?" Pip asked, startled that his own voice sang with the language of Faerie.

"Then it would be difficult for us all," Ælfstan said. "We are not of your world, and you are not of ours. Our leaders will not allow humans in Faerie, and we must stop our kind from coming here. So I will help to secure the power of the wall before more of our kind are pulled through."

"What can we do to help?" Pip asked.

"You must stop the darkness from spreading," Ælfstan said, then sat back and gazed into the depths of Merlin's fire. "And then," he said, eyes still ablaze with the reflection of green flames, "and then you must find someone to rule."

Nine

Looking north, Pip scanned the countryside before them—out toward the lands that led to his old home. He never thought he'd see home again. Still, they were many miles from the Caledonian Forest and Mordred's old fortress. The company of magi-soldiers and mages had regrouped in Aquae Sulis and had now been traveling along the old Roman road for nearly a fortnight. Merlin had called the road the Fosse Way, and Alfred had tried to give Pip a lecture on Latin afterward. Pip had tried to listen at first, but then rolled his eyes. He was good with magic and a bow, but he was as likely to master Latin as he was to become a battle mage.

He'd been practicing with the elements and could put fire into his blade without melting it. Niall had given him another sword and had been testing him every time they made camp. He was enjoying sword practice with other magi-soldiers and mages. He thought he might be getting better. And Merlin had taught Pip the spell so he could understand all foreign tongues. The spell was extremely complex and seemed to last no more than a day, but if he wished to communicate with the hobgoblin, he had to use it. And so he did.

Alfred had refused the spell, claiming he would rather suffer the rigors of learning a new language than having spells placed upon him.

Privately, Pip thought Alfred didn't enjoy spell casting and, as a magus, had no desire to learn a complex spell. Regardless, Alfred had gotten better at working with magicking pages to incorporate plants. He could even send Merlin messages from one spelled parchment to another across the camp. Despite not being a mage, Alfred's skills in magic were growing.

They'd journeyed on the road from Aquae Sulis and now stood on a low hill that faced the city of Lindēs in the distance. Merlin, Ælfstan, and Niall rode up alongside Pip and Alfred, and together they gazed out over the landscape of forest and farmyards yawning before them. The green land lay desolate. The soil rested. Farms lay forgotten, their fields fallow.

"There was once a great Roman fortress in Lindēs. The Romans thrived here. Thousands upon thousands of them," Merlin said, pointing toward the city.

"Yet there's no one here." Pip surveyed the too-quiet farm and took a deep breath of the still, weed-tinged air.

"They're here. Hiding, most likely," Niall puffed, eyes scanning the horizon. "I have little magic, yet even I can sense some darkness." He rubbed the toe of his leather boot into the earth as if to ground out an ember.

"Hopefully we will sway some to our ways," Alfred said.

"Who will farm? Who will tend the shops?" Pip asked.

The breaking of the realms had seemed like the right thing to do at the time, but Pip hadn't considered the consequences. Their existence, their very world, had been turned upside down. Maybe now the mages left behind would realize how important the non-magical had been to their civilization. Before they'd left South Cadbury for the north, Merlin had spent months working on a secret project that might give them a bridge between the Earth Realm and the Magic Realm. He called it the Key Stone Portal. Merlin and Pip had found no success, so Merlin had instead been working to link the Key Stones within the Magic Realm so they could more easily travel from one part of the realm to another. Pip still wasn't certain if it would work.

"The magus will have to do all the work themselves. They will have no choice but to rebuild since they no longer have slaves to do their bidding." Merlin scanned the barren landscape, eyes darkened. "Evil is like a weed. Pluck one out, and others will sprout up and take its place."

"But Mordred's gone," said Pip.

"Aye, he's gone. But we must be vigilant. Niall is right. There is darkness here, and it's flowing from north to south. Those who followed Mordred still linger. The dark mages will regroup. They will all be vying for power. And with Mordred gone, there is no one to stave off the invaders from the north."

"Who will take charge? Without Arthur, we have no king." Alfred's cheeks flushed pink in the breeze, and he swallowed back an expression of fear.

"Then you must find one," croaked Ælfstan as he nibbled on the last bit of hardtack. "In the meantime, I will travel with you, help you secure the wall for the sake of my realm and yours, and then you can find a way to send me home." The hobgoblin inclined his head to Merlin.

"The Aurelian Council will rule until a new king emerges." Merlin seemed to have an answer for everything. "And we will accept no one inclined toward the dark ways, be they Christian or druid."

Pip hoped that whoever the would-be king was, he'd soon be revealed. He didn't like the thought of a leaderless land or the threat of the dark magus joining with the Northmen. "And what of Mordred's kingdom? Who will lead that?"

"It is my hope that our new king will take charge of all the kingdoms in this land," Merlin said. "That he will use the stone circles we have been working on to remain vigilant about the goings-on of this vast kingdom. For now, we must rally the mages. We will create alliances and form a powerful presence to protect the north in Mordred's stead, and then we will determine who is to be king." Merlin smiled in a way that made Pip think he knew more than he was saying.

Pip was about to ask how they would determine such an important thing when the sky quickly darkened and heavy clouds moved in.

A rumble of thunder boomed overhead, and fat raindrops stung Pip's face. Niall held up an arm to signal a stop to the line of troops. "Let's camp here for the night. We will scout Lindēs after the storm passes. Ready tents." Niall's voice rumbled nearly as loud as the thunder, sounding frighteningly like Bowan's.

The buzz of activity was fierce. The soldiers and mages, all trained to care for themselves in the field, sprang into action, unloading their packs and readying tents.

Pip suddenly wished for Mistress Adella, the plump cook who'd accompanied him on his journey to South Cadbury. His heart twinged. His sister, Mary, had worked with the cheerful cook, but they'd both been taken from him and placed in the Earth Realm. He hoped Mary was happy and that Mistress Adella was fully recovered from the injury Mordred's bandits had given her. He supposed he'd never know. Even if Merlin discovered the spells necessary to visit the Earth Realm through the Key Stone Portal, Pip would never be allowed to go. That privilege would be reserved only for Merlin and the new king.

Pip shoved away the longing thought of his family and turned to more pressing matters. Hunger. His stomach rumbled in response to his thought. As soon as camp was set, they could eat. So he'd better help. Da always used to say, "Many hands make light work."

Some men cared for the horses, while others set up the leather tents, twelve in all. Eight soldiers to each of the ten larger tents, and two smaller ones were erected as well. One for Merlin, Pip, and Alfred. One for Caraline and Gwenn. Pip and Alfred helped a soldier with the smaller tents, while Gwenn and Caraline worked on a meal with Merlin.

Before the tents were fully up or the meal prepared, the spattering of rain turned into a torrent. Sheets of cold, blinding rain pounded them. Pip and Alfred finished setting up one small tent, but the other lay folded in its pack.

"No time!" Merlin called and gestured for the boys to lead their horses to where the soldiers were sheltering their animals in a copse of trees nearby. "The animals will have shelter and food enough. But we must seek refuge."

A blaze of lightning lit up the heavens from crown to earth, and a tremendous boom shook the ground.

"There'll be no attempt at fire in this supernatural tempest," Niall bellowed. "Hard tack and cheese. In your tents—"

That's all Pip heard before another crash of thunder drowned out the huge magus-soldier's words.

Damp and chilled, Pip was annoyed that their tent built for four would house six this evening. He'd been so busy practicing with the elements and sword and spells that he'd barely spoken to Gwenn, but now she and Caraline and even Ælfstan would sleep with them. Not that it was their fault. He and Alfred had managed to erect only one tent before the storm came so unexpectedly, and Gwenn and Caraline had no place to shelter. Ælfstan, who'd been sleeping outside for much of the journey, now huddled with them.

"Hobgoblins don't like the rain," he sniffled, and a large drop of water spattered down onto his nose from his great, floppy ear.

Pip sighed. At least they were safe and mostly dry.

Still, the tent was musty and cramped, and his belly rumbled. Somehow Caraline looked content. After rubbing her hands in a small circular motion, a tiny light flared in her palm. It glowed soft and green and emitted a soothing warmth. "Well, this will be a cozy night. A good time to discuss your studies and get to know one another better, yes?" She gave Gwenn a meaningful nod, and Merlin cast the language spell on Caraline and Gwenn so they would understand the hobgoblin. Alfred, however, refused the spell again, saying he'd rather learn the language.

Caraline passed out hardtack and cheese, then unwrapped a small package she had tucked in her cloak. "I was planning to put these in the stew, but since we'll have no fire, we might as well enjoy them." She unwrapped the little package, revealing several dried mushrooms.

Ælfstan scrunched his massive nose and scooted backward as if the smell offended him. Merlin chuckled. "Don't like mushrooms?"

"Shaman elves use them for seeing. And, no, I find their stench appalling." Ælfstan grimaced as Merlin popped one in his mouth and chewed.

"These are fully edible and have no mind-altering properties," Caraline said, then offered a few dried fungi to Pip, Alfred, and Gwenn. "Are you sure you wouldn't like to at least try one?" She offered Ælfstan a tiny sliver, but the hobgoblin scooted away with a grunt, making them all laugh.

"It's not funny," he said in his croaky-hoarse voice. Pip offered Ælfstan the biggest piece of hardtack. The hobgoblin took it in his long, gnarled fingers and nodded his thanks.

After they ate and had taken turns sipping rainwater from a small bucket Merlin had set outside, they relaxed around Caraline's mystical green fire. Lying back, Pip was warm and content, his belly full. He watched the tiny green flames dance and flicker yet burn nothing. The sound of heavy rainfall pattering against the tent made him drowsy.

Alfred sat close to Ælfstan and Merlin. Ælfstan would say a word, Merlin would tell Alfred the meaning, and then Alfred would repeat the word in Faerie. Every few minutes, Ælfstan would have Alfred repeat all the words he had learned. Pip was impressed at how quickly Alfred memorized the words and their meanings. After listening to them for a bit, Pip turned his attention to Gwenn and Caraline.

Caraline had a small leather-bound book open before them, its pages covered with drawings of various plants with Latin names written beside them. "You can use certain herbs to enhance your powers. They can help you control your transformation."

"But can they help me better blend with the shadows?" Gwenn asked.

Caraline thought for a moment. "I believe there is a spell to help with disguise. It won't make you invisible, but it will help you blend with your surroundings. With your talent as a shifter, it could be extremely useful."

"I'd like to learn that." Gwenn gave her aunt an eager smile.

"I'll need to look through my notes and confer with Merlin, but I'm sure we can help you with it." Caraline and Gwenn continued to talk, and Pip lay back and listened.

Merlin and Caraline were both powerful in magic and in knowledge. And with Alfred and Gwenn, and even Ælfstan, perhaps together they would make everything all right. Perhaps the loss of his family wasn't for nothing. He'd fought so hard to find them, only to give them up so they could be free. And now that the people were free, he wouldn't let the dark mages or these Northmen take that from them. The cost had already been too high.

He sighed, letting the sounds of their voices, soft against the rain and thunder, soothe his heart. Feeling safe and content, his eyes grew heavy. Yet as soon as they closed, Pip awoke in Halfdan's skin, half-naked and covered in blood.

Ten

The sticky warmth of Halfdan's blood oozed from the thin slice in his arm. Pip could feel the dull pain of the injury as Halfdan squeezed his fist, allowing blood to flow into a silver chalice set upon the stone altar before him.

Through Halfdan's eyes, Pip saw they were in a modest stone building, likely a church abandoned because of the Northmen. It was dark except for the candlelight that glowed pale yellow, tossing shadows on the stone floor where three overlapping triangles, which Halfdan knew as a *valknut*, were drawn in charcoal. Black mist seeped from the pale stones. It twisted and began to rise. Taller and taller it grew as Halfdan chanted.

Halfdan thrust the chalice toward the vortex of darkness swirling at the *valknut's* center. "I call upon my fallen ancestors! I call upon the slain! Rise, lord, and let me serve you! I call upon you, Loki! Come forward so I may do your bidding." The chalice clattered to the floor, the blood evaporating into the darkness that began to take shape.

Halfdan slumped forward, his breathing ragged. The price for calling a god would be heavy; he could feel it in the marrow of his bones and in the depth of his soul. He only hoped that Loki would answer him in this new land.

A towering form of blackness loomed above him, anger roiling like a crown around his head. "Halfdan Ragnarsson." The unearthly voice rumbled, making Halfdan's bones ache.

Summoned to rise against his will, Halfdan rose to kneeling before the darkness. His eyes traveled upward until he could make out the rough outline of a massive, barbed, skeletal ribcage. And, finally, to the angular horned skull. Large, empty eye sockets gazed down at him, an eerie flame-like glow flickering where the fleshy orbs should be.

"What are you?" Halfdan's voice didn't quaver, only his eyes held a hint of fear.

"I . . . am . . . sent by Loki." His blackened lips curled back into a cruel smile. "I am Beli. Adversary of the Christians, friend of those in *Niflheim*, and of Surtr and Hel. I will bend to do your will . . . for a price."

"There is always a price, great prince." Halfdan inclined his head, but kept his fierce blue eyes on the beast Loki had sent.

Beli grinned, jagged teeth jutting between soot-black gums. "Then what do you ask of me? And I will tell you my price."

"Land. Gold. Power. I want a kingdom in these new lands. My kingdom to rule as I choose."

"A kingdom of darkness." Beli's growl sounded almost like a purr.

Halfdan dipped his head. Yes, a kingdom where he would worship his gods and sacrifice as he pleased. He needed not only to please Odin, Thor, and Freyja. There would be no more interference from the *gothis* who sought only *Valhalla* and *Folkvalgnr* and *Helgafjell*. The afterlife. They seemed to care nothing for the power that could be brought to this life from the dark realms like *Niflheim*.

Halfdan reached into his fur-lined cloak and withdrew a heavy gold chain, one he'd claimed last season as part of a raid to the east. This would be a good payment.

The cool metal was heavy in his hands. It could buy him land and sheep and rich cloth. It would please his wife. But instead, he offered it to the demon.

Beli studied the exquisite chain of gold that Halfdan held before him, but then he scoffed. "What use have I of gold or silver or jewels, Northman?" His eyes blazed. Halfdan didn't have an answer for him.

"I want your soul," the demon said, dark mist twisting around his horns. "And the soul of every male heir that descends from you. And then you will have your kingdom. You will have power. And you will have many sons. Many heirs."

Halfdan's eyes widened. His sons? His heirs? Was he willing to offer his future children, his children's children, his own blood? For land? Riches? Power beyond his wildest dreams?

Of course he was. He would stop at nothing for power.

Throwing his arms wide, Halfdan opened himself to the beast. "With my blood and soul, I accept your offer."

Pip startled awake, the feeling of icy cold blackness retreating from the pit of his chest where the demon had reached out to touch Halfdan. Pip opened his eyes, ready to tell Merlin what he'd seen, but found Ælfstan staring down at him. The hobgoblin's face shone greenish-blue in a sliver of pale moonlight that streamed through a small gap in the tent.

A scream barely escaped Pip's lips before Ælfstan placed a knobby finger over his lips for silence, then beckoned Pip forward. Ælfstan let out a gravelly word, which Pip could barely understand, the language spell beginning to fail. "Follow."

Having slept in his clothing so he'd be ready at a moment's notice, Pip scrambled up, pulled on his boots, and followed Ælfstan through the tent flap into the damp night.

Merlin was already there, looking over the dark landscape. The rain had ceased, but the air was wet, and Pip could hear droplets falling to the earth from the surrounding trees.

"What is it? What's happened?" Pip asked the master mage. Pip looked back to the tent, but no one stirred. Not even Alfred was awake.

"Come with me, but don't wake the others. Not yet." Staff in hand, Merlin led Pip and Ælfstan through the sleeping camp and into the dense forest of trees that surrounded them.

After a few moments of walking, their feet tamping down bracken and slick leaves, they reached a clearing at the edge of a low ridge that looked out onto the expanse of flatland.

Dotted across the green fields like ravens flocking together were the tents of dark mages, their auras barely concealed. Flashes of tired greens and browns and oranges swirled with the gray energy of their dark ways, flaring from the tents where they slept. Brighter auras, also flecked with gray, moved about the camp as the guards on duty patrolled. The place reeked of darkness and anger, and coupled with what Pip had seen from Halfdan, he knew that if these mages joined with the Northmen, there would be nothing but death to their newly freed kingdoms.

"It's as if we're looking into a pit of Hell," Pip said, knowing he'd best tell Merlin about what he'd seen. They couldn't let the dark mages, Halfdan, or his Northmen take over the lands they had fought so hard to free. So Pip took a deep breath, ensured no peeping eyes or hidden auras were nearby, and told Merlin and Ælfstan what he had seen of Halfdan and the blood sacrifice. As they listened, the sky turned from gray to purple to pink with the waking of the sun.

Ælfstan nodded. "The Christian Hell. The Norse Hel. They are different, but neither good. Yes, this gathering of dark mages is a gateway to death. But light can overcome dark. Surely Merlin has taught you this." Ælfstan looked at Merlin, whose worried eyes surveyed the scene before them.

After observing the enemy camp, Merlin finally spoke. "I believe we have found what's left of Mordred's mages. And those we spotted outside of Aquae Sulis have likely joined them."

"There must be two hundred soldiers there," Pip said, trying to count their numbers as best he could. "Some dark battle mages and many magi-soldiers." At least there were no slave soldiers. Pip's stomach turned rancid at the memory of having to fight those Mordred had enslaved, Pip's own brother, Galen, included. These dark mages were bad enough, but at least they were fighting of their own free will, which meant Pip would feel less guilty if he had to kill them. But he would do it if he must, to help keep the kingdom free. "But we're outnumbered by more than two to one."

"And I fear we have found more than mere dark mages and magi-soldiers, as you call them," Ælfstan said, his voice barely a whisper. He pointed a long finger toward the encampment. "Look there. Do you see that banner with the snakes on it?"

Pip squinted until he could make out a black banner with two snakes circling one another in the shape of an S, each attempting to eat the other's tail. "I see two serpents. What does it mean?"

"'Tis a symbol of the Northmen, I believe. But I don't know what it means," said Merlin.

"Death and trickery," said Ælfstan. "I need not know what it means. I can feel it. There are others here from an unfamiliar land."

Pip reached out with his senses, but could not feel Halfdan. There were dark mages in the tents and in the camp, their sickly energies twisting about them. Yet none here felt as powerful as the northern jarl who would be king, nor as powerful as Mordred had been.

"I don't sense their leader, Halfdan," Pip said. "But if some of his men are already here as you say, then I fear the dark mages have already chosen a new leader."

"And you say Halfdan called for a god named Loki?" Merlin looked as troubled as when he'd been worried for King Arthur's life on the battlefield at Badon.

"Yes." Pip nodded. "But instead of Loki, a horned creature came. He called himself Beli. Halfdan opened himself to the demon, or whatever it was. The creature's fingers were like ice. They reached out for him. And then I woke. But I think the Northman has taken on the power of some strange god—or demon."

"Alfred will say the one true God is on our side and that with Him we cannot be beaten," Merlin said. "But I hear your concern, lad. And I, too, fear these unknown gods and the ways of these strange Northmen."

Pip found safety in Alfred's steadfast beliefs. He, too, believed in the Christian God, but Pip knew there was power in the druids' beliefs. And so, too, there must be power in the beliefs of the Northmen, despite their differences.

"Let us hope and pray that Alfred is right," Merlin said, then turned back toward camp. "The sun will be up soon. We must wake the others and dispatch a message to Bowan. We will need more mages and soldiers before we can face them, and much sooner than I had expected."

After a hasty breakfast of dried fruit and more hardtack, Niall ordered all the soldiers packed up and ready to march. While the men quickly and efficiently broke down the tents and readied the horses, Merlin summoned a meeting.

Merlin gathered Pip, Alfred, Caraline, Gwenn, Niall, and Ælfstan beneath a great old oak tree, and leaning on his staff, he addressed them each in turn.

"Niall, march the men east-northeast. Go carefully. Avoid the dark mages, and send scouts ahead to see what we have yet to face."

"These will go north," Caraline said, gesturing toward the enemy encampment. "From what I scried with the runes, I believe they intend to join with the Northmen."

"You're certain?" Merlin asked.

"I am. I don't know where, but they will move north. Somewhere near the wall. The Northman Pip has seen attempts to draw power from it."

Ælfstan hissed. "The fool will destroy it and send all manner of creatures into this world."

"Pip, you, Alfred, and Gwenn will stay with Caraline," Merlin said. "Remain close to the dark mages as they travel, but stay hidden. Caraline, work with Pip on his sight. Gwenn, use your powers of transformation to discern what you can of the Northmen's plans. Alfred, provide counsel and record all you learn and see. Once you've discovered where this group intends to go, meet Niall in Eoforwic."

"But where will you be?" Alfred squeaked.

"Ælfstan and I shall attempt to travel by stone portal. I had not finished my work on the stones before we left South Cadbury, but I've done enough that we can travel quickly to alert Bowan and our mages to the threat massing in the north. They should be in Winchester by now. It will take them time to travel north as the stones can only transport one at a time, and it is not meant as a method of troop transport. It must remain secret."

Merlin must trust Ælfstan to talk about the portal stones in front of him. Gwenn, too, Pip thought. He hoped the trust wasn't misplaced, but the hobgoblin seemed to want to protect the wall from destruction. And Gwenn was with Caraline, and Pip trusted Caraline. Gwenn spoke little, but she could be helpful in spying on the dark mage camp and the Northmen.

"Gather your things, learn what you can, and meet me in Eoforwic in two days' time. That will give us time to prepare and plan before we confront Halfdan. I foresee a great battle ahead, one that will determine the fate not only of our realm, but of the world."

Part Two
Born from Steel

Eleven

As the pinks ebbed from the sky and the sun's pale yellow light illuminated the puffy white clouds above, Pip watched Niall lead a trail of horses and soldiers away from him in a single line that left nothing but muddy hoof prints. Merlin and Ælfstan had already departed to a nearby stone circle to quickly get to Bowan in Winchester, leaving Pip with Alfred, Gwenn, and Caraline and their horses. The camp had been broken down except for a single tent that slept four.

Pip shoved away the uncertainty that wormed around in his gut about being left by both Merlin and Niall. He'd been on his own before, had faced bandits and dark mages, but Bowan or Niall or Merlin had always been close by. This time they were going to different parts of the kingdom—away from him—leaving him to a mission of his own, and he didn't know if he was ready for the responsibility. Caraline was powerful with herbs and medicine, but she was neither a warrior nor a mage. Neither were Gwenn nor Alfred. Pip alone would have to protect them. And he must protect them. Alfred was the closest thing Pip had to family. Besides, Caraline had always been so kind, and Gwenn reminded Pip of his sister. He would let no harm come to them as he had his mother. He would control his power, and in so doing, he would discover the mage he was meant to be.

"We must settle on a story in case we're discovered," Caraline said. "Something simple so we won't forget if we're nervous."

"Displaced farmers, perhaps?" Alfred suggested. "I know little about farming, but we've seen so many abandoned farms along the way that it would make sense."

"Agreed," said Pip. "A likely story, I think. And everyone else knows something of farms, yes?"

Gwenn nodded. "I lived on a small farmstead, and my mother grew herbs. I can do that."

"I helped Da with chores and animals, and I used to hunt to help put food on the table," Pip said, remembering how much he used to love to run through the forest with his bow, battling imaginary foes and seeking dinner. He'd loved his bow and arrow then; now his feelings were mixed. A sword was definitely better in battle—at least in close quarters. He just needed to find one that felt right in his hands. He gripped the sword gifted to him by Niall to replace the one he had melted. It was balanced and not too heavy, but still felt clumsy in his hands.

"It's settled then," Caraline said, smiling. Pip noticed it was a tight smile, not her usual carefree one. "We are displaced farmers, and you are my niece and two nephews. Your parents gone as well."

That part, at least, was true.

"Right," Pip said. "Let's follow the movements of the dark mages and learn what we can of their numbers, their power, and if they have already joined the Northmen."

"And I can creep into camp as a cat to lap their milk and learn their secrets." Gwenn's eyes sparkled, and Pip realized how valuable a cat sìth could be. She could literally turn into a cat, skulk into camp, and spy on anyone. The thought made him shiver. He was glad she was on his side.

Without another word, Gwenn's body shook and trembled, and before their eyes, she transformed into a sleek black cat. She purred and twisted around Caraline's ankles.

"You'll not go to that camp alone," Caraline said to the feline as if she were scolding a small child.

Pip nearly laughed at the sight, but managed to hold his mirth. Even Alfred let out a giggle.

"I'll go with her," said Pip. "I need to assess the mages' auras and try to discover what power the Northmen have." Gwenn stared up at him with the same large green eyes. "See if you can find out what they're planning—especially if there are Northmen here."

Merow. Gwenn gave a chirp of understanding.

Before Gwenn could prance off, Caraline scooped her up and held her nose to nose. "Do be careful, Gwenn. I know they won't know what you are, but if anything happened to you—"

"I'll look out for her," said Pip.

"See that you do," said Caraline, and she set down the squirming Gwenn. "Alfred, you and I shall not stray far from the camp or our horses, but we shall go collect plant specimens for your book and berries so you can make spelled ink. Merlin would be most disappointed if all of you didn't learn something from this excursion."

Keeping low and staying close to the forest undergrowth, Pip had to trot to keep up with Gwenn. She moved quickly in cat form. Black and low to the ground, she easily blended with the shadows of the landscape.

Pip cast a concealment spell over himself before leaving the safety of the trees, then paused at the edge of the small cliff that overlooked the enemy camp.

"We need to count the tents to get a better idea of the numbers. We need to know how many dark mages, how many magi, and how many Northmen," he told Gwenn, who had paused beside him. "I agree with Ælfstan. From my sight, I think there are already some Northmen here."

The camp below bustled with life. Dark mages practiced spells, sending sparks of green and orange into the air. Some practiced archery, their arrows creating thin tendrils of darkness that left splotches of blight on the trees where they landed. Pip watched with fascination as the trees' auras flared bright green, their own power fighting to overcome the darkness of the arrows. He hoped they'd heal.

On the far edge of camp, Pip saw a circle of rough-looking men with strange clothing and axes. Their auras were dark and tinged with silver and red.

"Look," Pip said. He picked up Gwenn, who squirmed and gave

him a yowl. He pointed her nose in the direction he wanted her to gaze. "Just look." He pointed down at the strange long-haired men. "That group there doesn't look like us at all. They must be the Northmen."

Gwenn looked, then hissed at him.

"Okay. I'll let you down," he said, setting her by his feet. "Just be careful, Gwenn. We don't know if they might wield some strange power that lets them see who you really are."

A cry rang out suddenly from the trees behind them, distracting them from the enemy camp and making them turn toward their own. The cry had come from somewhere near their tent.

Gwenn startled, but Pip crouched low and laid a gentle hand on her. "Quickly, into the scrub," he said, pointing toward a small, dense copse of trees with a good vantage point. "We don't know what it was."

Lying hidden in the overgrowth of vegetation, they could see the open field of the dark mages' camp. Soon, at a low spot on the cliff, a small band of dark magi-soldiers emerged leading a prisoner. Pip could tell they were magi-soldiers and not full mages because of the green sashes they wore, and he knew they were of the dark because black instead of silver runes were embroidered on their clothing.

A low growl sounded from deep in Gwenn's chest. The fur on her back bristled, and her ears flattened. She was ready to attack.

Pip looked closer at the prisoner the soldiers were escorting to their camp, and his heart fell. Now that the group was in the clearing, he could easily see the prisoner's forest green cloak and strands of auburn hair floating in the breeze.

"Oh, no. They have Caraline—"

Gwenn let out another deep-chested growl followed by a *hisssss*.

Pip's heart ached. No! They couldn't take Caraline. He'd promised to keep her safe. He'd promised! He had to save her.

Pip leapt up, sword in hand, energy flaring. But Gwenn raced in front of him, and his heart nearly choked him. She could be seen and caught, too. Every fiber of his being screamed at him to charge down the hillside, attack the dark mages, and rescue Caraline. But where would that get him? He remembered what had happened when he'd raced after his sister. Alfred had needed to rescue him from a pit of corpses at Mordred's camp. No. And when he'd charged to save Alfred at Aquae

Sulis, he'd lost all control and melted his own sword, rendering himself powerless to help. He would not make the same mistake again. He would be smarter.

"No, Gwenn! Stop!" Pip scooped up the feline and ducked back into the brush. "I want to save her, too, but we can't just charge in there without a plan. We have to think. And we need to find Alfred. Then we'll come up with a plan. We'll get her back, Gwenn. I promise."

Pip tried to soothe the cat, but she spat at him, bit his hand, and then, without so much as a backward glance, she shot off into the dark mages' camp alone.

Pip lay in the brush watching the mages take Caraline into camp until he saw Gwenn's feline form disappear among their enemies, and his gut twisted with shame. He should be with her, but he would be outnumbered. At least he knew where they were. Now he needed to find Alfred so they could plan a rescue mission.

Pip made it back to what was left of their camp by midmorning. It was eerily quiet. The horses were gone, as was their tent—likely taken by the magi-soldiers who'd taken Caraline. He had nothing. No shelter. No rations. No water. And where was Alfred? Pip hadn't seen him with the magi-soldiers.

Opening his senses, Pip scanned the camp area for auras. The trees shone their usual green, and small bursts of gold and purple flared where animals hid in the underbrush. He sensed no scouts, but no Alfred either.

"Alfred?" he called as loud as he dared, lest some scout farther off hear his voice carried on the breeze. "Alfred, you can come out. No one's here but me. It's safe."

A branch cracked overhead, and Pip looked up. He immediately saw Alfred's aura, which flared gold with streaks of frightened gray, then his eyes focused on the green cloak that marked Alfred as magus and helped him blend with the young leaves.

"Come down," Pip said, annoyed with himself for not looking up.

What if a dark mage or magus-soldier scout had been up there? He'd have been caught or killed for sure. At least it was just Alfred.

"I—I'm stuck." Alfred's voice quivered.

"Stuck? Just move back to the trunk and come down the way you went up," Pip said, reminded anew at Alfred's frailty. He spent so much time with books and quills and ink that he didn't get enough exercise.

Pip walked to the base of the tree and looked up to where Alfred clung to a large branch. Leaves crowned his head, twigs sticking into his hair. His cloak was caught in branches on either side, making him look like a large bat with green wings. Despite his concern for Caraline and Gwenn, Pip tried not to laugh. "Just set your foot on the next lowest branch."

Alfred hugged the tree harder, his eyes squeezed shut, the gray in his aura lighting up Pip's vision like lightning. "I—I can't . . . I'm afraid of heights."

"Then how'd you get up there in the first place?" Pip asked.

"Caraline used a spell and magicked me up here," he said with a scowl. "As soon as we heard the soldiers, I told her to hide, but they had already seen her. She didn't give me a choice, or I'd still be by her side."

"And you'd be captured along with her," said Pip. "I saw them take Caraline, and Gwenn's gone into the dark mages' camp on her own."

"She did? Without a plan?" Alfred slipped down to the next branch. "Ouch," he said, still hugging the tree. "I thought maybe . . . I thought Caraline would escape. Why did Gwenn go after her without us?"

"I told her we needed a plan first." Pip sighed, then shrugged. "She's stubborn. She was in her cat form, and she bit me. I wanted to go after Caraline, too, but we would be outnumbered. Once she finds Caraline is safe, maybe she'll come back to us with information."

A rustle nearby made both boys freeze. Alfred hugged the tree harder, and Pip drew his sword.

Suddenly, a chittering squirrel launched itself from the bushes and scampered up a nearby tree. Pip let out a sigh, thankful it wasn't a man or even one of the man-squirrel creatures he'd accidentally created when he was learning to wield his power.

"We need to get out of sight and make a plan before it gets dark," Pip said.

Alfred looked down at Pip, then shut his eyes again and squeezed the branch tighter.

Pip's temper flared, but he forced himself to be calm. He asked himself, *What would Merlin do?* Merlin would likely float Alfred out of the tree with magic the same way Caraline had put him in it, but Pip didn't know a spell for that. Unless he floated Alfred like he'd floated water when he first started studying with Merlin. He shook his head. Alfred was much heavier than water, and if he fell, he could get hurt. No. He had to do this without magic.

After what felt like hours, Pip had Alfred sitting in the crook of the oak about six feet above the ground.

"Now all you have to do is climb down the trunk, and you'll be on the ground. Then we can eat," Pip said, as much to his growling stomach as to Alfred.

Alfred clutched his satchel tightly to his chest, pulled his cloak snuggly around him, and peered down at Pip. "What if I fall?"

"Then you'll land in a bed of leaves," Pip said and began pushing brown leaves from the autumn past into a pile below the tree. A sudden howl from a nearby cluster of trees sent shivers down Pip's spine. Pip threw back his head and moaned. "Alfred! We need to get to safety. We can't stay out in the open all night. The dark soldiers could come back, and if they do, they'll see us, even if I keep my aura tamped down. And we need to make a plan to get Caraline back. So turn around, put your foot on the tree knot there," he said, pointing to a spot about two feet beneath Alfred, "then drop to the ground."

Another howl. Gooseflesh coursed over Pip's arms, and he drew his sword. At least he'd had that on him when their camp had been raided. His bow and arrows had been taken along with his bedroll, clothing, and horse.

"But you'd better hurry. I'm not staying out here all night." He gripped the sword in his hand, eyes skimming the woods for movement or auras.

"Do you see anything?" Alfred asked.

"Nothing," Pip said, scanning the forest that encircled them.

Alfred let out a long sigh. "Oh, fine. I'd better do it then. If I don't, I know Master Merlin will make me train with you and Niall."

"Maybe he ought to," Pip said. Alfred needed to learn how to protect himself, but his arms were so skinny that Pip doubted Alfred could even lift a sword.

To Pip's surprise, Alfred suddenly turned around, missed catching the gnarled tree knot with his foot, slid unceremoniously down the rough tree bark, and landed in the pile of leaves.

Uff.

Pip extended a hand, helping Alfred to his feet. The young scribe brushed crushed leaves from his cloak.

"Are you okay?" Pip eyed several scrape marks along Alfred forearms from where he'd clung to the tree.

Alfred glanced at his arms with a shrug. "My satchel protected my front on the way down, and your leaves protected the rest."

"Well, I'm glad you managed to keep ahold of that," Pip said. "You still have rations?"

Alfred nodded. "Caraline was teaching me about different plants I could use to help enhance the spells in my ink. So I had my bag with me. I've got rations, my waterskin, a spare cloak. Of course I have my parchment, ink, and quills." Alfred's voice trailed off, and his eyes welled with tears. "I'm sorry they took her. I'm sorry I couldn't protect her."

"There were too many of them, Alfred. Even if Gwenn and I had been here, there were too many. And it sounds as though they took you by surprise."

Alfred nodded, then looked away, hastily wiping his cheeks.

"We'll get her back." Pip awkwardly patted the skinny scribe's shoulder. "It's good you kept your satchel. They took everything else."

"Everything?" Alfred's eyes widened in alarm.

"Everything." Pip nodded toward a small animal track that disappeared into the trees. "There's a good place for us to hide just this way, and we'll make a plan to rescue Caraline."

Twelve

Golden rays of late-afternoon light pierced the clouds, playing soft and warm on Alfred's face as he scribbled a magic note to Merlin with special ink Alfred and Caraline had spelled. Pip hoped Alfred's magic worked and the note reached Merlin immediately. Then he'd know about Caraline's capture and the growing enemy threat.

Alfred chewed his lip in thought before writing something with a flourish. Pip had learned to appreciate Angel Face. He was a good and kind and true friend. He'd risked his life to help find Pip when he'd been taken by Mordred's men. Pip had hoped and prayed that the strife would have ended with Mordred. But while his family was free, his land and the people were not. They truly needed a king to unite them all.

Now Pip had a decision to make: leave Caraline and Gwenn behind to go north with Alfred to meet with Niall, or go find Gwenn and try to free Caraline—sending Alfred on alone. Pip's stomach twisted in knots. He didn't know what to do, but he had to decide.

And to decide, he needed to move. So he climbed out of the enclosure they were using as a hiding place, and after ensuring no spies were about, he started pacing. What could he do? What should he do? Niall had always said that action helped him think, but pacing wasn't doing

Pip any good. Well, one simple thing he could do was check their camp to make sure there were no new footprints. So he quietly began to walk around the camp.

He breathed in the afternoon air, which smelled of oak and pine. Tiny leaves, just sprouting green and new, swayed in the cool breeze. Spring was here, and the frost, it seemed, was gone for the season.

Pip left their hidden copse of trees and slowly walked around the small clearing where they had camped with Caraline. Aside from the many boot prints and hoof marks Niall's men and horses had left, Pip saw no prints of either a human girl or a cat's paws. Gwenn, he decided, must still be in the dark mages' camp with her aunt. And if she was there, he would have to find a way to draw her out as soon as possible. But how?

"Pip." Alfred's voice carried as a low, hushed whisper on the afternoon breeze.

"It's okay, Alfred. No one's here but us," Pip said. "Are you finished with the missive?"

Alfred climbed from their hidden space beneath the tree. "I sent it. Pray my spell worked! Have you found Gwenn?"

Pip squatted down, searching the ground for another moment, then shook his head. "No. Not even a paw print. No new sets of prints either." Pip rose and gazed toward the dark mages' camp. "We have to find Gwenn and get Caraline out."

"I know what you're thinking, and you can't just go dashing into the camp to find her! You could be captured, and this time Bowan isn't around to help save you," Alfred spat, his face crumpling. "And—and I'm not sure what I'd do without you."

The truth of his words stung, but Pip knew Alfred was just afraid. And Pip wasn't the same boy he'd been all those months ago—the boy with no control of his power who'd fallen in a hole and been wounded and captured. No. Now he was a mage, and while he may still struggle to control the flame with his blade, he was getting better at it. And this time he would be smarter.

"I'm not going to dash in to find Gwenn. I'm going to sneak into camp cloaked in magic. When I find where they're keeping Caraline, I'll wait until the guards have left their post and speak to her. Gwenn is bound to be nearby."

"Right. As I said, you're planning to go dashing into camp on a foolish rescue mission. I didn't even go into Mordred's camp. I stayed on the outskirts watching for you. Going into their camp . . . You're mad." Alfred stood up fully, attempting to smooth his tousled blond hair.

"I'm not mad. I'll use the concealment spell Merlin taught me. I've been working on it."

"And what am I supposed to do?" Alfred wrung his hands, looking thoroughly terrified.

Pip knew Alfred didn't want to seem cowardly, and in truth, he wasn't a coward. Alfred was brave. He just wasn't built for fighting or sneaking about behind enemy lines. "I need you to stay at the tree line and watch. If you see us flee, join up with us. If not all of us get out, then meet with those of us who do. I'm going to free the horses—"

Alfred's mouth popped open. "Free the horses? First you want to rescue Caraline, and now you want to steal horses?"

"They're *our* horses. The dark mages stole them from *us*. So it's not stealing as much as it is taking back what's rightfully ours. Besides, you don't actually want to walk all the way to Eoforwic, do you? It would take us a sennight on foot. On horseback we can be there in two or three days."

Alfred opened his mouth, then closed it and gulped. "I don't like it."

"You don't have to like it. I don't like it, but it makes the most sense. We can't abandon Gwenn and Caraline, and we can't walk all the way to Eoforwic." He jutted his chin toward the dark mages' camp. "Even if we walked, they'd likely overtake us on the way." He shook his head. "As much as we don't like it, it's the best plan. So watch for us and the horses, and be ready. Merlin needs us to meet him in Eoforwic."

After setting a concealment spell over Alfred in a dense patch of undergrowth with a view of the enemy camp, Pip moved closer to the edge of the cliff where he could make his way down. First, he dirtied his cloak with dried leaves and sticks, then rubbed a bit of dirt on his face for good measure. He then cast a concealment spell on himself so he could more stealthily sneak into the dark mages' camp.

He lay flat on his belly at the edge of the cliff, studying the movement of the dark mages, soldiers, and Northmen. They didn't appear to be packing up to leave, so what were they waiting for? Or for whom?

The dark mages' camp bustled with morning activities. There were definitely at least two hundred men: magi-soldiers, dark mages, and a small band of Northmen. They gathered in small groups around several campfires.

Many of the soldiers nibbled on some sort of flatbread and dried fruit. Pip's stomach growled. At least Alfred had still had some food, but they'd finished that off this morning. He'd have to find something to eat once he got into camp.

Barely able to see his own arm thanks to his spell and twig-strewn cloak, Pip stayed low and crept down the rocky hillside toward the enemy camp. He could see no one behind the tents, which were set up in a circle with a wide trench running all the way around the periphery. There were no palisades or ramparts in place, and only a few magi-soldiers stood guard. They must not be concerned about Merlin or any of Arthur's remaining mages or soldiers to be so lightly guarded.

Pip grinned—that would make sneaking in even easier. He pulled his energy inward like a ball of yarn and spun it into the center of his chest where he guarded it from view with the mental wards he'd been practicing. Then, with a big exhale, Pip crept into the dark mages' camp.

Pip moved through the throngs of stinky soldiers, most of whom hadn't bathed in weeks. He was so close they could reach out and touch him, but with his spells in place, their eyes skimmed right past him. They stood around mending clothing, sharpening swords, or eating breakfast. No one seemed to notice him, which gave him time to observe the camp up close. The magi-soldiers' tents were in rings around the outside of camp, but in the center were the tents of the dark mages, officers, and, it seemed, the Northmen. At least that's how it sounded from the boisterous, foreign-tongued songs that flowed from a few tents near the center.

Pip followed the singing and, coming around the corner of a tent, found several large men and a few women with fair skin and long blond hair plaited in various styles. Strange, swirling tattoos covered their hands and arms, some even wrapping up around the backs of their necks. One of the Northmen oozed power, which radiated from him like the summer sun. His tattoos were the heaviest, and he spoke seriously to one of the dark mages. Suddenly, a set of sharp blue eyes—cold, powerful eyes—flicked up and met Pip's.

Pip felt an explosion in his chest, like his energy was being yanked out of him. Like he was being measured and tested in a glance. Pip immediately ducked behind a tent, but his heart thundered in his chest. Had the strange blue-eyed Northman seen him?

A strange, deep horn sounded, and there was an uproar of voices. Had he been seen?

He had to find where they were keeping Caraline, and fast. Pip snatched his aura even tighter and scurried to the center of camp.

Two guards stood before a single tent, but no others were being guarded. That must be the one. As he approached, he saw a black feline body, followed by the swish of a black tail, slither beneath the tent wall. Gwenn!

Skirting the guards by going around a neighboring tent, Pip crept up to the prisoner tent from behind. The deep horn sounded again, and the energy around him changed. The magi-soldiers and mages were no longer at ease, but on alert. He had to get out of the open—and quickly —lest a powerful mage see though his cover spell or glimpse his tamped-down energy.

Finding the small gap where the cat had slipped inside, Pip dove to the ground between the securing ropes and quickly pulled himself beneath the leather tent and out of view.

Inside, the light was dim. He immediately sensed two people and saw their auras of green and silver. Caraline and Gwenn. Even without seeing them clearly, Pip knew them from their energy. One of healing and love, the other of quiet, friendly trickery. Their hushed voices stopped, and they immediately turned to look at him.

"It's me," Pip whispered, creeping closer. Excitement burst through his veins in small pulses, and he had to force his happiness at finding Caraline down to a dull beat.

Gwenn gave a small mew.

"Pip?" The tent was too low to stand up in, but Caraline reached forward and pulled him into an embrace. "What are you doing here? It's too dangerous. If they knew of your power, of your connection to Merlin—"

"Well, they don't." Disappointment laced his voice, and the excitement he'd felt at finding Caraline and Gwenn dimmed. "There is no way I was going to leave you here. We need to go. Now."

"Where's Alfred?" she asked in a whisper.

"Safe. He's in a secluded patch of trees that I've spelled with protection and concealment. It's not far from where we camped the night before you were taken."

Pip went to untie Caraline's hands, which she held behind her back, but they were already untied, the ropes loosely coiled to trick the guards in case they checked. "Gwenn untied me, but they check often."

Gwenn's feline form quivered, but Caraline gave her a fierce look and shook her head. "No, Gwenn. There is commotion out there. Stay in your cat form. Pip, have you been seen?"

Pip scowled. "Not seen exactly, but one of the mages, a Northman, read my energy, I think."

"That's not good. They may know you're here. They are heathens and perform blood sacrifices beyond even the druid rites. Sacrifices that give them unnatural power. You must go and take Gwenn with you."

Gwenn hissed, and Pip spoke. "I'm not leaving without you."

"You must. The best way you can help me is to find Merlin. They won't harm me. They don't see me as a threat, but as a gift for their leader, their jarl. Halfdan Ragnarsson." Caraline seemed resigned to her fate, only a faint glimmer of hope remaining in her aura.

The Northman from his visions. The one who had summoned a demon.

"What else do you know?" Pip asked, slipping the loose rope from Caraline's wrist, despite her annoyance.

"They've been scouting for other dark mages that were still scattered in the area after the Breaking."

"The Breaking?" Pip asked, watching Gwenn, who was peering warily through a small gap at the front of the tent.

"It's what they're calling what you and Merlin did to break our world from the ordinarius. But they received a summons—just last night—from their jarl. He's forming an army, and they want us to move north. To Pons Aelius."

"That far north? That's Mordred's old territory. Why?" Old fears of Mordred and the pain of losing his home still lingered in Pip's chest, but he realized they weren't as strong as they once were. He wasn't so much afraid of going north as he was of another evil ruler taking control.

"The Northmen have offered the dark mages and their soldiers land and leadership. They have all agreed to be ruled by Halfdan Ragnarsson, a powerful Northman mage, if they serve him," Caraline said.

"Why would they want to serve him when they were just freed from Mordred?"

"Why do followers follow and leaders lead?" asked Caraline.

Pip didn't have time to philosophize. "You sound like Merlin," he huffed.

Caraline gave him a small shrug. "They want to be rid of the remnants of Arthur's realm and everything he stood for. They want power. Wealth. Land. They want to worship their gods and practice their dark ways and not be ruled by mages of light. Halfdan has promised them as much."

"Then we must go and warn Merlin and the Aurelian Council. Niall and Bowan need to know, too." Pip tugged Caraline to her knees and motioned toward the small gap he'd used to slip into the tent.

"I don't have your power. They'll see me," Caraline hissed.

"They won't!" Pip knew that by casting a new spell, his aura would flare, but it didn't matter. He wasn't going to lose Caraline or Gwenn. He was going to protect them. He took a steadying breath, focused his energy, and surrounded Caraline with a protective cover spell.

Caraline's eyes widened as Pip's aura blazed with magic. "No, Pip. They'll see you!"

"There!" A loud voice boomed outside the tent. "A bright light."

"Go!" Pip said shoving Caraline toward the gap. "The spell will hold until you're safely away. Find Alfred."

"What? Where are you going?" Her voice cracked in panic.

Gwenn meowed urgently at her aunt as if to say, "Hurry! They're coming!"

"Follow Gwenn," Pip whispered. He would stick to the plan he and Alfred had devised. But no matter what, he would fight to protect his friends. "Go. I'll be right behind you. I have to get the horses first."

"They'll capture you!" Caraline cried.

"They'll capture us all if you don't go. Go with Gwenn and find Alfred. Now go!" Pip shoved Caraline, sending her toward Gwenn, whose green eyes peered urgently beneath the tent. Even if he were caught, it would be worth whatever punishment he might receive. He refused to let Caraline or Gwenn suffer the same fate his mother had.

"Just be quick and be safe," Caraline said, and she hurried to follow Gwenn out of the tent.

Just as Caraline's feet disappeared beneath the tent wall, the front leather flaps burst open. Pip had no time to renew his cover spell, so he flopped onto his belly and dove beneath the leather flap, right where Caraline's feet had disappeared. The old concealment spell should hold until he could free the horses, at least against the magi-soldiers and weaker mages. He was halfway through the opening between the tent wall and the ground when a pair of rough hands grabbed him by the legs and yanked him backwards.

"Gotcha!" a rough voice said.

Pip was pulled back inside the tent. In one swift movement, a large magus-solder had set him upright, and Pip found himself looking directly into the face of the fierce blue-eyed Northman.

Thirteen

The blue-eyed Northman mage spoke with strange words, which were translated by the magus-soldier. "What is your name, boy? And why did you release the woman?"

"Alfred," Pip lied, giving the same name he'd given when he'd been captured once before. True names had power, and he wasn't about to give them his own. The Northman's eyes squinted as though he knew Pip wasn't telling the truth, but he waved away the answer. "Why are you here?"

"I didn't want you to harm her," Pip said. His magus-soldier captor translated his response, and the Northman grunted, crossing his arms over his chest.

A dark mage joined them, and the questioning continued. Who was the woman? Was she his mother? How many had he traveled with? Of course, Pip didn't tell the truth; they didn't need to know about Gwenn or Alfred. Or that they were going to meet Merlin.

Finally, after what felt like hours of questioning, the Northman mage waved his hand in annoyance. "He's full of lies. This boy's no farmer. Look at the marks on his hands—those are from weapons practice." The Northman spoke with halting words, but Pip could understand him.

"I want to see your power," the Northman mage said. "It is balled up in your chest like a knot of rope, and I think you are far more than what we can see."

The magus-soldier squinted at Pip, then spoke to one of the dark mages who had joined them. "I see nothing," said the soldier, who still bore Mordred's old black standard.

"You wouldn't," spat the dark mage. "You're not a full mage." His dark eyes bored into Pip's, and tendrils of dark energy flowed from his fingertips, invading Pip's chest, probing around his heart like some strange instrument in Merlin's rooms at South Cadbury.

Pip silently pulled his aura into a ball tighter than yarn wrapped on a drop spindle and hid it in his heart. The rhythm of his blood pumping through his veins intensified, as if his heart were imbued with magic. He prayed his magic would be concealed there. Prayed that his heart would not explode from so much power in such a small space. But he had to hide it. If they knew he was a full mage, if they knew of his power, they would either force him to join them or kill him.

The dark mage probed and prodded Pip's mind, seeking some spark of magic. Sweat beaded on his forehead, and his eyes bulged with effort. Finally, the man grunted, and his dark tendrils of power retreated. "I feel something, but nothing strong. Nothing nearly as strong as you, Ivan." The dark mage nodded at the powerful Northman.

The Northman, Ivan, continued staring at Pip, his icy blue eyes calculating. Words flowed from his lips in the same strange language Pip had heard Halfdan Ragnarsson speaking in Pip's dream-walking. Pip couldn't understand their meaning, but he suddenly felt drowsy, as if Mother had given him an herbal tonic because he was unwell.

Pip struggled to stay upright, but his head fell forward as if a lead weight had been placed inside his skull. His eyes drooped, and he felt himself falling. And falling and falling. Yet he didn't hit the ground. He was floating on clouds of blackness. Suddenly, an icy blue light, the same as the Northman's eyes, pierced the darkness.

He tried to run. To hide. But there was nowhere to go in this abyss. The light would find him, and then he would be shown for what he was. A true mage.

Pip curled in on himself, cowering in a ball like one of the terrified children he'd seen at the markets where they'd sold ordinarius when Mordred had ruled.

That's when the light found him. It was warm at first. It grew warmer and warmer and then bore into him like a searing hot beam. His body spasmed, and he screamed and screamed. He would let the pain take him, but he would never—*never*—show his power. He would never turn on Merlin or his friends.

After what felt like an eternity, the intense pain slowly receded. Pip was vaguely aware that his body was being moved. He felt his face against a rough plank of wood, the swaying of travel by cart, and the coolness of the air. Pip heard the cadence of soldiers marching and the clomping of horse hooves. Yet he was not awake. Not to the mortal world. He knew he was dream-walking, but he didn't know how.

He reached into himself, feeling for the tightly wound spool of power held in the center of his chest. It was still there, dimmer now, like the embers of a dying fire, but there. Contained. Safe. He stared into the embers, watching the flickering intensity of his power. He could see shapes. Familiar human shapes. They moved through a dense wood. Then they were in a large encampment. He heard laughter tainted with fear.

Pip focused harder on the shapes. It was Caraline, Alfred, and Gwenn. They were surrounded by hundreds of magi-soldiers and mages. But not dark ones; he could see from their auras they were light. His friends were safe, and his heart rejoiced. They'd made it! He was captive, but they were safe.

Yet how long had he been captive for them to travel all that way? It felt like mere moments, yet the darkness of the abyss and the pain of the cold blue light could have been an eternity.

He swooped as if a winged creature and peered down at them from above. A massive stone, part of an ancient stone circle, stood at the center of their camp. He saw Niall and the hobgoblin, Ælfstan, standing next to it. They made a strange pair. One tall and thick muscled, the other short and hunched. Together they stared at the large stone as if waiting for something.

Pip swept closer. Runes flared with the colors of fire, dancing along the rock's surface. The great stone made a humming sound, and Niall stepped back. Suddenly, as if the face of the stone were a liquid pool, Merlin stepped through, followed by Bowan and a few other mages.

Staff in hand, Merlin surveyed the camp. He took a few steps forward to greet Niall, but stopped, then cocked his head as if listening to something. Slowly, he turned to look straight at Pip!

"We know where you are, lad, and where they're taking you. Hold firm. We are coming for you." As Merlin spoke, he aimed his rowan wood staff at Pip, and a jet of silvery purple light coursed around him. He fell from the tree, but not downward. Backward. As if a wind of power propelled him farther north. Away from his friends. Away from Merlin. Away from safety.

Pip's heart ached that Merlin had pushed him away. Why would he do so? But he held fast to the great mage's words. *We are coming for you.* He would believe it. He had to. Yet he couldn't fight the gentle wind that pushed him northward.

The purple light faded, and the wind ceased, and Pip found himself settled on another stone. This one in a Northman's camp. But not any Northman. At the center, Pip saw Halfdan Ragnarsson.

Pip moaned awake, the straw beneath him poking through his shirt and into the skin around his ribs. His head pounded as if he'd been struck by a millstone, and something pulled annoyingly at his hair. *Ouch!* He swatted at the twinge of pain, and his hand met with a feathery body and sharp beak.

Caw. Caw.

Pip twisted around and stared into the dark, pearly eyes of a large female raven with sleek black plumage.

Caw.

"Well, hello to you, too," Pip said, quickly checking to ensure his power was still deeply held within him. Sure that it was safe, Pip slowly sat up, rubbed the sleep from his eyes, and tried to smooth down his hay-strewn hair. The bird cocked her head at Pip as if expecting him to say something. Instead, Pip lay back and closed his eyes. His power was well guarded, and his head hurt too much to get up.

The raven cawed again, pecking Pip's head so hard that he forced himself upright, despite the pain. "What is it—" He stopped, his heart aching for the bird. The raven's left wing was broken and stuck out at an odd angle. "Oh. You poor thing," he said. Seeing no humans nearby, he made a tiny crack in the armor he'd placed around his power. From the crack, he pulled out ultra-thin threads of golden energy and wrapped them snuggly in his fist.

He lifted his hand so he almost touched the raven, who simply cocked her head and peered curiously at him. "This might pinch a bit and feel warm," he told the bird. "But then you'll feel better." He opened his fingers and directed the energy so it flowed from him into the broken wing. Pip could see his golden light entwine with the raven's purplish aura. The bird gave a startled cry, but didn't move away.

Pip watched as both energies threaded themselves together, weaving around sinew and muscle and bone until the wing was whole again. Slowly, his golden light seeped into the raven's aura, then settled deeply into the creature's bones.

Pip lay back with a satisfied sigh, resealing the energy within. It'd been too long since he'd used his powers to heal. At South Cadbury it'd been all sword training and spell casting, potion making and dream-walking. At least now he felt he'd actually done something good.

Despite his aching head, Pip knew he wouldn't fall back asleep, so from his heap of fresh hay, he looked around at the long structure he was in. The roof appeared to be made of grass and the walls of wattle and daub, but it differed from any building he'd seen before. There were several horses in nearby stalls, and he heard the cluck of chickens. He must be in some sort of barn.

Caw. The raven pecked at his head again, urging him to get up.

"Oh, all right," Pip said. "I might as well find out where we are. It's not like you'll let me rest." He slowly climbed to his feet and peered out a narrow window cut into the wall.

Caw, the bird called again. Stretching her wings, then fluttering up to land on Pip's shoulder, the raven gazed out the window with the young mage.

Pip saw he was in the middle of a busy camp. A Northmen camp. The men and women had long, strangely plaited hair, and tattoos covered their muscular bodies. Most carried axes and swords. There were warriors everywhere. And in the distance, he could see a massive stone wall. If what Gwenn had heard about the Northmen camping in Pons Aelius was correct, then that must be the old Roman wall—Hadrian's Wall—and beyond it, his old home. A pang of longing twinged in his heart. For an instant, he wished he could escape from this barn-like prison, rush through a broken opening in the wall, and travel until he reached the small house he'd shared with his family. But Mother was dead and buried, and Da and Mary and Galen were enjoying their new life in a new realm.

The raven, still perched on his shoulder, nuzzled his head affectionately. "We're surrounded. So it looks like I won't be going anywhere anytime soon," Pip murmured to his feathered companion, scratching the bird at the nape.

"And where would you go, young mage?" came a heavily accented voice, sending the raven fluttering to the rafters. "There is nothing but the wall to the north and my scouts to the south. You would not get very far."

Pip turned with a start and found himself face to face with a heavily muscled, powerful man. His aura radiated some gray light, but was mostly dark and tinged with crimson. He wore leather like a Northman, and at his side was a wicked iron sword inscribed with strange runes. His dark blond hair was pulled back in a style Pip had only seen in dreamwalking, but Pip recognized the icy blue eyes. This was the Northmen leader, the jarl. The man who vied to be king of the north. He was Halfdan Ragnarsson.

"I—" Pip began. Where would he go? If given the chance, he'd find a way to Eoforwic, to his friends. But he didn't even know where he was.

The jarl gave Pip a savage smile. "You're in my camp at Pons Aelius," he said, as if he'd read Pip's thoughts. "It's heavily protected, so don't try to run lest you're ready to meet the gods."

"There is only one God," Pip said, surprised at himself for confronting the big man.

"My gods will prevail," Halfdan Ragnarsson said simply. Crossing his arms over his chest, he walked to one of the slim windows that let in a stream of light and fresh air. "My fortress is already under construction, and many warriors here—magi-soldiers, I believe you call them—have joined with my men, as have some of your land's most powerful mages. And yet my spies tell me there are some who mount forces against me in the south." He turned his icy gaze back to Pip. "The question is, young mage, which side are you on?"

Pip stood there defenseless, weighing his options. To tell the truth —to say to this fierce, strange warrior who'd made a blood pact with a demon that he meant to drive him, along with the darkness, from their lands—would mean certain death. To lie and go against his true intentions would surely tarnish his aura, which he felt slipping from his ironclad grip since he'd cracked it open to heal the raven. Halfdan Ragnarsson already knew he was a mage; he'd said so. But Pip hoped he didn't know the extent of his power. He needed to bide his time. Merlin said they were coming. Pip needed to survive and learn as much as he could about these strange invaders without his aura betraying him.

"I—I haven't decided," Pip said, giving thought to the void of power in the north and to what Halfdan Ragnarsson might offer.

The large mage studied Pip for a long moment, his cold eyes searching Pip's. Finally, his snarl broke into a boisterous laugh that made the animals stir and the raven squawk above. "I like you, young mage. You have a warrior's spirit," he said, tousling Pip's already messy hair. "They tell me your name is Alfred, but I don't believe it." A hint of ice flashed in his eyes, but he didn't stop smiling. "Come to my hall with me. We shall eat and drink and talk, and then I will decide what to do with you."

Pip didn't dare attempt an escape from a camp filled with Northmen mages, magi-warriors, and the dark mages Halfdan's men had collected from the south. If Pip tried to run, he'd certainly be captured. So Pip followed the jarl from the long barn-like structure he'd been in to an even longer building with a thatched roof.

Halfdan led them through a massive set of oak doors that opened into an immense room with a welcoming fire. The fire crackled in a long trough-like hearth that ran down the center of the hall, and on either side of the fire were long tables with benches where warriors ate and drank. Pip saw no children, but many muscular, weaponed men and even women who wore knives at the hips of their kirtles. Pip wondered what Niall and Bowan would think of women fighting in war, and if they faced one, would they strike or try to capture their opponent.

"Sit." Halfdan Ragnarsson commanded Pip to take a place at a table just below a raised platform at the head of the hall where two throne-like chairs were placed. Halfdan sat in one of the high chairs, and beside him in the other sat an elegant but fierce woman with a powerful, blazing aura of gold, crimson, and darkness. Black tattoos danced up her neck, making her look even more foreign and fierce than her strange clothes. Pip knew it was Halfdan's wife and that she was a powerful sorceress.

Under the watchful gaze of Halfdan and the sorceress, Pip sat. A plate full of roasted chicken and vegetables was placed before him, along with a tankard full of something that smelled faintly of honey. He was too hungry to refuse the kindness of these strange people, even if he didn't want to be ruled by them. As he ate, he listened to the familiar accents of the dark mages along with the strange language of the Northmen that filled the room. The noise and bustle was strange, yet soothing. The laughter and songs lifted his spirits. Pip stuffed fingers full of greasy meat into his mouth. The meat was savory and unusually spiced, but good. It would be nice to have a leader again. Stability. Normalcy. But from an invader? Pip swallowed the last bite, wondering if the Northmen were as bad as he'd imagined from what he'd seen.

Wait. What was he thinking? Halfdan Ragnarsson killed his own brother. Of course they were as bad—at least, this one was.

Suddenly something warm and soft rubbed against his shin. He looked down to find a black cat with bright green eyes looking up at him.

"Gwenn?" he whispered to the floor. "Is that you?"

Merow.

Pip's heart danced with relief and joy and terror. Gwenn was here! She had found him!

"If they catch you," he murmured. "Ouch!"

She nipped his ankle, and he immediately saw that a dark mage sitting across from him was staring. "Who are you talking to, boy?"

"No one, sir," Pip said, terror striking his heart. He pulled a piece of roast chicken from his plate and dropped it near his feet, and Gwenn devoured it. "Just a barn cat."

Gwenn hissed at him.

"Well, doesn't like you much, does it?" the dark mage said with a laugh, then turned back to his companion.

Pip tossed Gwenn a few more pieces of chicken, then bent down, pretending to pet her head. "Tell Caraline I won't try to run. I'll learn what I can and meet up with you when the time is right," he whispered.

Gwenn looked at him as if she wanted to speak, but of course she couldn't.

"Don't worry," he murmured. "I'll be careful. Now get out of here before they catch you. I've heard Northmen sometimes use cat fur for coats!"

At that, Gwenn gave a low growl, then tore out of the tent.

Certain that Gwenn was safely away, Pip finished his plate and was offered another. With a warm drink and fully belly, he felt himself relaxing—and the grip on his aura slipping. Immediately, several eyes were on him.

He cinched up his aura, hoping the icy-eyed jarl hadn't noticed the slip. Yet when he glanced to the high seat where Halfdan Ragnarsson sat, the cold blue eyes were locked on him, as were those of the strange sorceress.

"The boy has power, Halfdan. You should make him a thrall," bellowed a fat, drunken Northman mage who sat across from Pip. Then he belched so loudly that those around him erupted in uproarious laughter. Pip could only tell the Northmen mages from the magi-warriors by the intensity of their auras, and this man's was barely more than a warrior and had the color of vomit.

"I want to rule these lands, not have slaves. There will be plenty more time for thralls when those who refuse my rule succumb to us," Halfdan Ragnarsson said, his eyes never leaving Pip. Thralls? Slaves? The food soured in Pip's mouth and curdled in his stomach. They kept slaves!

"And if they do not join us," Halfdan Ragnarsson raised his voice to a bellow, "then they will fight us!"

The hall erupted with great cries of fierce joy. Auras flared. Fists thumped tables. Toasts were made. These people loved fighting. These people kept slaves. Pip suddenly realized *his* people could be in even greater danger than they had been when they'd faced Mordred.

Pip's grip on his aura again began to slip, but this time it was not from the comfort of warm food or sweet drink. This time it was from the rage that boiled his blood. He'd fought alongside King Arthur and Merlin to stop Mordred from keeping slaves. He'd seen what the horrors of slavery could do and felt the pain of having his own family ripped from him. If he were killed in this hall, then so be it, but he would no longer contain his power. He would unleash it upon Halfdan Ragnarsson and his men and do whatever it took to stop them from enslaving the people of Britain—even if it cost him his life.

As Pip rose to his feet, his power simmering in his blood, the large doors of the hall were flung open, and a Northman scout rushed in with panic in his eyes. There was blood on his face, dripping from a gash across his forehead.

The voices and merriment in the hall died, and the scout approached the high chairs. "Jarl Ragnarsson." The man gave a courteous nod but did not bow as one would to a king.

"What news, Sigurd?" Ragnarsson asked, his attention averted from Pip.

Pip struggled to control his surge of anger and power; his veins felt alight with it, but he pulled it back as if reigning in a horse running for its life. He couldn't give himself away as a powerful mage. Not yet. He must show control. He must learn what he could and then escape to find his friends.

"We are being attacked. A large group of mages and warriors is on the march from Eoforwic. They will be here within the day." The man took a gulp of ale that was offered to him, but stayed on his feet to address the jarl.

"And who leads this group?" Halfdan Ragnarsson asked.

"A powerful mage they call Merlin."

Fourteen

"Prepare for battle! Make Thor proud!" Halfdan Ragnarsson brandished his sword in the air, and his words were met with an uproarious cry. None of them seemed to carry the fear of death.

Merlin! Merlin was almost here, and he came with troops. Obviously Alfred had reached him with news of the Northmen. Thank goodness! Pip hoped Caraline had reached them and that Gwenn would join them soon. In the chaos of cheers and shouts, perhaps Pip could sneak away and find his friends. Looking beneath the arms of several mages and warriors who were on their feet with excitement, Pip saw Halfdan was deep in conversation with a dark mage as well as some of his own Northmen. Now was his chance.

Ducking down, Pip crept beneath the long oaken table, then crawled toward the long hall's open doors. More Northmen warriors and even some magi-soldiers bearing Mordred's old emblem swarmed into the hall. Pip left the cover of the table, and like a fish swimming upstream, he emerged against the crowd of oncoming warriors.

Heart racing, he was almost to the double doors, but a wall of people was streaming inside. He just had to push through them.

Suddenly, a hand came down hard on his shoulder. "Not so fast, boy." It was the drunken Northman mage who had proposed Halfdan Ragnarsson take Pip for a slave.

With a scowl, Pip stomped as hard as he could on the fat man's booted foot, then kneed him in the groin. The big man groaned, but instead of doubling over in pain, he slammed the hilt of his sword into Pip's face.

Everything went dark.

Pip's head throbbed, and blood smeared his vision from the small gash above his right eye, but he was lying on soft bedding. Fur pelts tickled his skin, and a warm fire danced against his back. Through blurry red tones, Pip could see he was no longer in the main hall but in some private chamber. So as not to make the throbbing worse, he tilted his head gently to the side and saw a merry fire in the small hearth behind him. Yet the fire's merriness didn't go past the hearth as the flames sent fierce, nightmarish shadows dancing across the room's fur-draped bed, desk, and wooden walls.

Halfdan Ragnarsson stood before a small table in deep conversation with a massive dark figure, who Pip thought must be a dark Northman mage. The big man's aura was like black ice, dense and cold. He'd never seen such a black aura—not even Mordred's was so vile. Pip shivered despite the fire.

He tried to make out the words the two men spoke, but their voices were deep and strange. Pip wiped the blood from his eyes and strained to see the dark figure that loomed over Halfdan. Through the shadows, Pip's eyes began to make out the form, and he realized it wasn't a man at all, but a hideous beast. Where there should have been flesh was a huge skeletal ribcage with spikes along the ribs. The hands were like massive, clawed skeleton fingers. And, finally, he saw the head: a horned skull with large hollow eye sockets that glowed crimson. His char-black lips curled to reveal sharp, jagged teeth.

"Halfdan the Conqueror," the massive creature said in a loud voice that made Pip's insides fill with dread. "That shall be your new name as conqueror of this new land."

Pip knew at once this was the same creature he'd seen when he'd dream-walked. It was Beli. The demon sent by the pagan god Loki from the dark Northmen realm of the dead. The one to whom Halfdan Ragnarsson had sworn a blood oath.

Pip tried to be still, but his power flared at the threat, and two sets of hostile eyes turned to regard him.

"Ah, you're awake," Halfdan said. "And now I can see where your true allegiance lies." He stepped toward Pip, inspecting the boy's aura. Pip winced under the scrutiny, but with his head wounded, he could not keep his energy masked from the evil jarl.

"He is a mage of light. Young, but powerful." The demon swung his distorted bony face back to Halfdan. "And you were too blind to see it. You should have destroyed him," Beli growled, his eyes flashing red. "Perhaps I misjudged you when I offered you such power."

"You did not misjudge me," spat Halfdan. "I could sense his power." Halfdan stared at Pip with his icy gaze, as if weighing the young mage's power and thoughts. "But he has better control than most his age. He is one of the people I hope to rule. He could be helpful." Halfdan gave a half-shrug. "Perhaps. I had hoped he would join me. I could use powerful mages from this land with warrior hearts."

Beli's snarl turned into a gruesome smile. "Then perhaps *I* can persuade him." With a rapid motion of his claw-like hands, bars of swirling gray and black energy slammed down around Pip. Pain shot through his head and twisted like a knife into his eyes. He cried out, but couldn't move from his spot by the fire. The bars caged him in place.

Beyond the physical pain came wave after wave of emotional pain. His chest felt as if it had been sliced open, and the guilt of everything he'd ever done wrong in his life crashed down on him like a massive stone: his mother's death, nearly killing King Arthur, tearing apart his family. Almost costing his friends their lives when he'd lost control of his power and melted the blade. The pain of uncertainty and doubt twisted a like blade in his heart, and black flames from the bars that caged him eagerly lapped at his skin.

Pip heard Halfdan and the demon arguing like an annoying buzz of flies. There were other voices in the room now, too. Loud. Frantic. The sound of explosions. Magic tinged the air. A horn sounded the alarm and shouts rang out, but Pip was in too much agony to understand what they said. Yet somehow he knew that if he was left in this torturous cage of darkness, he would either succumb to the pain and die or plead for his life and join Halfdan. He would be given no other option.

As if in response to his thoughts, the dark energy rippled over him, crashing deeper into his soul. He felt weak, helpless. A baby mage, not a warrior. The darkness plucked at strings of his energy as if it were a carrion bird pecking out the entrails from a carcass. It was as if the darkness were attempting to unravel the light from within. As if it were desperately seeking a way to plant a seed of evilness inside him.

No!

He may not be a great warrior like Niall, but he *was* a mage. He would not fail Merlin or King Arthur. He'd sacrificed too much. He'd fought too hard for the light and for freedom. He would not let the darkness have him—even if it cost him his life. He would never join Halfdan Ragnarsson. Ever. The bars around him seemed to grow thicker, closer. They tightened their grip on him, burning his skin until it puckered and charred. A cry escaped his lips, and his vision dimmed from blurry red to gray, but still he pushed his energy outward like a candle flame.

The pain tried to claim him, but he would never give in to the dark. He had wielded fire before, and he would wield it now. This dark power would not conquer him.

He threw out his energy wide, opening himself up to the light. To fire, water, earth, air, and all the energy in between. That's when he felt it—pure *draoidheachd*. The essence of magic. True power. It surged into him, filling him to overflowing. Then, his energy flared from him in a blaze of white and gold and orange. It danced with the dark fire, entwining itself with it, and Da's words came flooding over him. *Let your light shine in the darkness, and the darkness will not overcome it.*

All of Pip's energy streamed from him like life's blood. He gasped as blazes of white and gold consumed the darkness. His lungs tightened as if all his power had left him. His heart stuttered, and the darkness was swallowed by the light.

For a moment, everything was quiet, still. Pip longed to go into the golden white light, to become one with it. No more pain. No more struggle. It felt as if his spirit were lifting from his body, and a sense of peace and calm swept over him. He could rest now and see Mother again. Merlin would miss him, and Alfred and Caraline and Gwenn would as well, but they would be okay. Everything would be okay.

Just as Pip was about to let go, about to let himself be absorbed into the light, he saw the flutter of wings. A small figure glided toward him. *Could it be an angel?* Perhaps this being would guide him to Heaven.

He reached out his hand to greet the creature.

Caw.

It wasn't an angel. It was a large black raven! The same raven he'd helped in the stables. She bit his finger—hard—then nudged his arm with her head as if to say, "It's not time to go. You must get up. Get up. Hurry!"

The light around him dimmed, the pure *draoidheachd* snapping back into the ether, and Pip settled heavily into his body. He was still beside the fireplace in Halfdan's den, but Halfdan and Beli were gone, and sounds of distant fighting filled the air. The dark bars of energy had left char marks on the floor and on his skin, but they had fizzled out. Pip's skin glowed a soft golden white, and the marks healed before his eyes, leaving thin white lines of scars. Pip wiped away sweat and blood from his forehead, but the gash, too, was healed. He wasn't in pain anymore. He actually felt healthier, stronger than he'd ever felt before. He felt almost like a warrior. Almost like a battle mage.

Caw.

His raven friend called out to him and flapped to a small door Pip hadn't noticed before. The bird peered through the opening, then back at Pip.

Caw.

Pip scrambled to his feet, surprised at how steady and strong he felt. He had no weapons, but his power pulsed strength within.

Caw.

The raven hopped impatiently by the doorway.

"Is that a way out?" Pip asked.

The room was suspiciously quiet. No guards. No sounds but the crackling of fire in the hearth. He peered out the door and saw it opened to a small chamber that held boots and shields and a few swords. From there, another door stood open to the outside. Beyond it lay a field, which faced the back of the Northmen's camp.

Pip glanced over the swords and picked the best, although all were in need of sharpening or repair. He slung a scabbard over his shoulder and slid the sword home.

The raven cawed, urging him to hurry, then fluttered up to his shoulder and gave him an affectionate peck on the ear.

"Thank you for bringing me back," Pip said, realizing that without the raven's call he might have given in to death. "You are a true friend. But you need a name." Pip thought for a moment, looking at the raven's delicate, smooth feathers and intelligent eyes. "I think you're a girl. So I shall call you Gabriella, after the angel Gabriel."

Pip scratched the raven's head, then peered out onto the open field. It was strangely quiet—empty. The clash of swords rang out from the other side of camp. Perhaps if he snuck out the back and around the periphery, he could escape.

Sword in place, Pip wove a spell of concealment over himself and Gabriella, and strode quietly out the back of Halfdan's den and toward the field of battle.

The rear of the Northmen's camp had been left unguarded. With tents concealing the camp in the front and a forest shielding the rear, Pip carefully snuck around the remaining guards and pikes, making his way through the trench and away from Halfdan's camp. Knowing Gwenn and Caraline had gone to meet Merlin and Alfred in Eoforwic, Pip gave the fighting a wide berth and planned to walk south. If he walked quickly, he should find his friends in a day.

A sudden blaze of purple and gold sparks flashed in the sky, making Pip stop where he stood. Those were the colors of Merlin's magic. Merlin was here!

Pip teetered on the spot, hidden in a small copse of trees. If he continued south, he'd likely find someone to direct him to Eoforwic. Yet he could also encounter spies. If he skirted the battle, he'd need to keep his power ready so he could defend himself. And he could be caught again. But if Merlin and the army were already here, a journey to Eoforwic would be useless. Besides, they may need his help.

Gabriella pecked him on the head, urging him to make a decision.

"I don't know," he groaned. "I wish you could fly up there, see who's fighting, and tell me which way to go."

The bird tilted her head and stared Pip straight in the eye as if she understood his words.

The raven blinked once, a thin, opaque membrane momentarily covering her marble-black eye. In that moment, the world seemed to slow. Pip saw himself reflected in Gabriella's eye. He saw into the bird's being. Her energy. The very essence of her life. He saw her majestic purple aura and could pick out thin strands of his own golden light— the energy he'd used to heal her wing—which was now part of her. A stream of energy passed from the raven into him and back to her again. It was as if she shared some sacred part of herself as he had done to heal her. Then, with a ripple in her eye like a pebble being dropped in a pond, the stream of energy tied itself off, and Pip was again staring at himself in the marble-like eye.

Crawk! she squawked, then launched herself into the sky.

Pip blinked once. Twice. Then his entire world changed.

He was aware of his body, nearly invisible at the edge of the trees, his cloaking spell still firmly in place. But he also saw through the raven's eyes. And what he saw took his breath away.

Pip soared above the trees with Gabriella. Through their shared energy, he was somehow connected to her. He not only saw what she saw, but felt what she felt. Her heart soared at the pure joy of flight, at the thrill of having a healed wing strong enough to carry her through the air once more.

The world appeared so different through the raven's eyes. The colors were more vivid—the blues and purples seemed to glow. Even Earth itself seemed to have a translucent barrier, jutting out in parallel lines, then twisting back upon themselves to make loops. It was magnificent!

Gabriella flew beyond Pip's hiding spot, over the Northmen's camp, to a field where swords clashed and magic blossomed in great billows. Careful to dodge the explosions of sparkling fire, Gabriella could see what Pip would never have been able to see even if he had snuck close to the battlefield. From above, Pip saw the line where both sides met: Halfdan with his wild Northmen and the dark mages on one side; Merlin with Niall and Bowan and other mages of Britain on the other. Yet they were still outnumbered by hundreds of dark magus, Mordred's old mages, and Northmen. Where was the army Merlin had gone to summon? There were fewer than two hundred who stood for Britain and the light.

Halfdan stood tall with his hands outstretched, the shadowy form of Beli towering behind him. The power gathered within Halfdan as if Beli himself were feeding the dark Northman mage more power. Suddenly a flood of darkness flew from Halfdan's fingers. Like a great web, the darkness spread over the battlefield, and the first soldiers it touched screamed in agony, their skin cracked, then charred, then turned to dust.

Oh, no. Stay back! Pip thought frantically to Merlin, to his friends, to Gabriella.

Gabriella shrieked and flew higher, away from the danger, as Merlin raised his staff and summoned the power of light. A wave of brilliant gold and purple exploded from his staff in a concentric dome that shielded the Army of Britain and forced even Beli to cower.

Merlin kept up the dome, and Beli seemed to shrink. He was still horned and skeletal and grotesque, but he was somehow less fearsome than he had been. Merlin's arm quavered with exhaustion, but still the dome held.

The horned creature said something to Halfdan, which made him scowl, and in a vortex of darkness, Beli disappeared from the battlefield. Halfdan's power immediately lessened. He barked orders to nearby mages, and they scurried to obey.

A horn blew, and Halfdan and his army retreated toward their camp, leaving the Britons alone on the battlefield with the charred dust of their dead.

Fifteen

Careful to avoid the retreating Northmen and dark mages, Pip hurried south to join up with his friends.

Gabriella led the way. She'd circle ahead to see where the wounded Britons were retreating, then she'd circle back to him and give out a caw of encouragement. It was as if she were saying, *Hurry! Keep up! Hurry! They need you!*

Pip's vision switched between his own sight and that of Gabriella's. It was startling at first, but he quickly learned to toggle between the two. And at all times, he had a sense of the bird's location and the direction she wanted him to go. Through her eyes, Pip watched the mages and mages of light, led by Merlin and Bowan, as they slowly traveled to a camp they'd erected several furlongs to the south. Once they entered the camp, Pip saw a shock of auburn hair: Caraline. Alive and well and healthy.

Pip smiled, glad Caraline was safe. He hoped Alfred and Gwenn were safe as well, but couldn't see them from his raven's view. Then, not seeing where his own feet trod, he tripped and landed with a thud on his ribs. *Ufh.* He quickly pulled out of Gabriella's vision and refocused on the world around him.

He was lying atop a large tree root at the edge of a wood. Not far in front of him was the Britons' camp. He was almost there.

Gabriella flew overhead and squawked at him, as if laughing at him on the ground.

"I'm coming," he called to her with a scowl. Then he climbed to his feet, attempted to scrub the dirt from his cloak, and quickly made his way to the camp.

He hadn't gone more than a few hundred yards when an arrow hissed past his ear, lodging itself in the ground behind him.

"Halt!" a young man's voice rang out.

Pip squinted, then found the source of the voice—and the arrow. A young soldier stood with a companion atop a hill that ran along the front perimeter of the tents. Now that he was closer, Pip could see men building small siege towers and erecting more tents. Flags of crimson and deep blue, the colors of the new Kingdom of Britain, flew above the camp. Pip's heart soared, knowing he would soon be among friends.

With a deep breath, Pip released the stranglehold he'd kept on his energy since leaving the enemy camp and let himself relax into the pulsating power of his aura. He saw the soldiers step back, and wanting to ensure they knew he meant no harm, Pip held up his hands to reveal he had no weapons.

"I'm Phillip Gwynhoed, a full mage and servant of the light. Tell Merlin or Niall or Bowan I've come," he called, his voice booming over the hillside, powerful and deep. He was surprised that he now sounded more man than boy. More warrior than apprentice.

The young soldier spoke to his companion, who quickly disappeared. Pip stood where he was, hands relaxed at his sides, and waited.

With a loud *caw*, Gabriella swooped in a wide circle around the camp, giving Pip a glimpse of Merlin and Alfred scurrying toward the guards' outpost. Satisfied he knew they were making their way to him, Gabriella landed on Pip's shoulder.

As soon as Pip's identity had been confirmed by Merlin and an overly excited Alfred, Pip was escorted straight to the command tent where Bowan and Niall were discussing battle plans.

All of the tents were made of leather, but the interior of the command tent was draped in rich purple and gold linen and silk to keep out the wind and prying ears. Pip could see the magic pulsing from the material, which was imbued with protective spells. Shadows filled the tent, lit by oil lamps and tallow candles that illuminated a table with maps set in the center.

Gabriella clung to Pip's shoulder as they entered the command tent. She didn't make a sound, but her talons dug harder through the thick fabric his cloak and into the meat of his shoulder. "It's okay. They'll love you," he whispered.

Inside, Pip found himself being embraced by Caraline, slapped fondly on the back by Niall, and then hugged again by Caraline.

"You should never have stayed behind to save me." Caraline's voice was angry, but her aura threatened tears.

"But all is well," Pip said, hugging her back, still glad he'd helped her escape. "Merlin needs us all."

Caraline let out an annoyed sigh, but pulled him back to her again, too relieved to be angry.

Gabriella squawked at all of the people and the touching. She didn't like being indoors or being so close to so many humans. Not one bit. But Pip felt her desire to be with him was stronger.

"And who is this?" Merlin asked. As soon as his eyes landed on Gabriella, she stilled, and they gave each other a long, apprising look.

"This is my friend," Pip said. "Her name is Gabriella."

Swak. Gabriella nuzzled Pip's head and gave him an affectionate ear nip.

Merlin took a half-step back, held Pip by both shoulders, and looked him up and down. "And yet again you surprise me, Young Pip. Your energy has changed. You now have something of the raven in you."

Pip nodded. "We helped each other. Now we share sight."

"Raven sight," Caraline gasped. "It . . . it is as rare as the cat sìth. Perhaps even more so."

At the mention of cat sìth, Pip glanced around the tent and found no sign of Gwenn. "Where is Gwenn? Is she safe?"

As soon as he said her name, a black cat emerged from the deep shadows in a corner of the tent. In an instant, the cat transformed into the girl.

"*Barn* cat?" Gwenn fisted her hands on her hips and scowled at Pip.

Pip threw his hands up in self-defense. "I had to. I—They could have—"

Her scowl transformed into a laughed. "It's okay, Pip. I know. I'm sorry for biting you, but I'm hardly a barn cat. I was on another mission to gather information about Halfdan Ragnarsson for Master Merlin and Bowan, as well as check on you." She gave him a feisty grin.

"Gwenn has been incredibly helpful," Bowan said, giving her a rare grin.

"And she's quite returned to herself. To the girl I knew before the Breaking," Caraline said with an affectionate squeeze to Gwenn's shoulder. "But spying? Really, Merlin, do you think it's a good idea? She's so young."

"Of course it's a good idea," barked Bowan. "Who else do you know who can get into the enemy camp undetected?" He glanced at Pip. "No offense, lad. Alfred here has said how powerful your concealment spells have gotten."

"That's right." Alfred nodded at Pip. "He kept us hidden from the Northmen when they came looking for us."

"True. But no one will think twice about a cat," Bowan said as if having a cat sìth as a spy was the most natural thing in the world. "And she will be invaluable to the future king if we keep her secret safe."

"But if they find out what she's doing. If they find out what she is," Caraline said, worry evident in the twist of her hands and the spark of gray in her aura.

"They won't," Gwenn said. "No one knows of my abilities except for those in this room . . . and Master Kitchener back in Aquae Sulis. No one else in the entire realm knows. The Northmen and dark mages will never suspect a stray cat grazing on scraps. Besides, I'm quick and see well at night." She yawned, and Pip swore he caught a glimpse of feline in her.

"A cat sìth on our side could change the course of the battles to come." Niall's brow furrowed as he went back to studying the parchment maps on the table before him.

Merlin studied Gwenn. "It could change the course of history for our entire realm," he said. "We will train you well and keep you safe."

Caraline nodded, but Pip could see gray concern clouding her usually emerald aura.

"Tell us all what you discovered, lass," Bowan said, gesturing at the maps before him, a softness in his voice Pip had never heard before. Bowan was usually all barks and bellows. Then again, Pip hadn't seen him around girls.

The group gathered around the table, which Pip now saw held not only maps but battle plans.

"Halfdan has them preparing to abandon the camp," Gwenn began. "The ancient fortress within Hadrian's Wall is almost ready, so they're reinforcing its perimeter. They have moved a decent supply of food and water within the fortress itself, and they are planning to make their attack from there. Halfdan had hoped to have it secure before officially forming an army and attempting to secure these lands, but we've pushed his hand. Now he wants to pull in all of the dark mages he can along with the Northmen who arrived with him. He knows they outnumber us, but you make him nervous, Merlin. He didn't expect anyone would have enough power to push back his fierce warriors or his demon."

"More of our troops will come. They march as we speak," said Bowan.

"But will they arrive in time for the battle?" asked Pip. "He's got hundreds of dark magi and mages along with his Northmen."

Pip's question was met with stony silence. Merlin pulled at his beard, his blue eyes lost in a gaze that was fixed to a flickering candle flame. "Is this the demon you told me about?"

"It is," Pip said, remembering the fiery dream-like haze he'd been kept in while being tortured by the demon. "It's—it's the horned creature named Beli." The name came out in a whisper, as if he didn't want to speak it too loudly. He didn't want to accidentally summon the beast. "The same creature I saw when dream-walking. He's the one Halfdan summoned instead of Loki."

"Beli. Yes, I recall you mentioning the name." Merlin's eyes narrowed, and Pip could almost see his mind sorting through volumes of old, dusty records. "Alfred, I believe you did some reading on the demon, did you not?"

Alfred went over to one of the many trunks that lined one wall of the command tent, flipped open the lid, and sorted through rolls of parchment until he got to a large tome at the bottom. The book filled his arms as he hefted it out. He tottered over to the command table and let it fall with a *thunk*.

"Watch the maps," barked Bowan, yanking a map out of the way just before the book landed.

Alfred gave him a scalding look. "I will *not* hurt the maps." His words were clipped, as if he could hardly believe Bowan would have such a thought. Alfred opened the large volume and flipped through the pages. "Beli," he mumbled. "Yes. I found the name . . . somewhere."

"He's some Northman demon," Pip said. "He brings fire and pain."

"As do demons from many religions. All creatures are connected. On this side and the next. Our religions are merely a glimpse into another world." Merlin held up his hands, forming a square with his fingers. "Each religion is like a window through which we have different glimpses into unseen realms." Looking through the opening he'd made with his hands, he moved them left, then right. "We shift the perspective, and the entire view changes."

"Speak simply," Caraline said, glancing toward Niall, who appeared ready to fall asleep.

"Simply that each religion is like a window into another world that we can neither fully see nor understand. And each person's perspective, and each religious text, shifts the view depending on how we look at it. So this Beli may be a Northman creature as well as a Christian one with a different name," Merlin said. "But knowing his name may give us more power over him."

Alfred's attention was focused on Merlin, his finger frozen on a page of the thick text. "I think you're right, Merlin. This is what I found." He showed them a page with a drawing of a horned demon with claws. "I think Beli is the same as the Christian demon Belial."

"That's him," Pip gasped, looking at the drawing. The picture looked almost exactly like the demon he'd seen in Halfdan's camp and during the sight.

Merlin's eyes darkened. "If that is so, this jarl has aligned himself with a very dark and very powerful entity."

"Yet you scare him, Merlin," Caraline said.

"And we will stop him." Merlin's voice struck the room like soft thunder. His aura flared purple and gold, warm and thick; it wrapped around them like a deep embrace. "Together we will stop them all."

After a warm meal and much discussion of battle plans and warding against demons, a sleepy lull settled on Pip. He was content for the first time in days, and standing among these powerful, good people, he felt safe. At least for the moment. He still wasn't sure if he was prepared for a fight or to face Beli again. His arrows had landed killing blows in the battle against Mordred, and his control of the flame had grown. Yet he was still not the warrior Bowan and Niall wanted him to be. He was merely a new mage who followed battlefield orders—at least most of the time.

He only hoped that his power combined with Merlin's would be enough to send Beli back to *Niflheim* or whichever netherworld he had emerged from. Pip gazed at the illuminated faces around the table. At his teachers. His friends. His family.

Merlin's face and beard glowed golden purple, even in the candlelight. Bowan's battle-hardened face and deep-set eyes were serious but ready to lead an army. Niall's eyes, normally sparkling with laughter and jest, sparked with hunger to fight. Alfred's face was pale but steadfast, and Pip knew his friend would do what was required of him. Caraline looked calm, resigned to the coming battle, her aura like a thunderhead hazed with green before a storm. And Gwenn.

Gwenn.

She wasn't the same girl he'd first met in Aquae Sulis. Her power had grown along with her confidence. The green and gold in her aura radiated around her and twisted through her in a beautiful filigree of knots and swirls. No longer did she appear to be a meek, shy girl, but a strong, capable young woman with the power of a mage. And with her black hair and pale skin and green eyes, she was . . . she was exceptionally pretty.

"What, Pip?" she asked, her aura glowing a faint green. "Why are you looking at me like that?"

"You ... you have a leaf in your hair." He brushed away an imaginary leaf. Her hair was softer than he'd imagined, and the touch ignited unfamiliar feelings in the pit of his stomach.

Merlin called his attention. "What did you learn in their camp, Pip?"

Pip swallowed back the uneasy feelings that raced through his blood, locking his aura tight lest Merlin sense what he was feeling for Gwenn, and then he told Merlin and his friends everything he'd seen and heard in Halfdan Ragnarsson's camp. When his words were spent, he asked the question he'd been longing to have answered. "How did you arrive so quickly?"

"My new spell worked!" Alfred bounced with excitement. "Merlin got the letter I sent. He was already here with Bowan and the troops when I arrived."

"But how? Winchester is a long journey."

Merlin's blue eyes twinkled, and he gave Pip a mischievous grin. "Do you remember our work on the Key Stone?"

Pip swallowed back hope. Of course he remembered. After they'd broken the Magic Realm from the Earth Realm, they'd spent weeks and weeks working on the Key Stone to create a gate between the worlds. But each time they'd tried to cross through the stone, they'd simply come out in a stone circle in Britain. So it had allowed them transport within their own realm, but had never allowed them to cross to the Earth Realm. But all that work had stopped in preparation for their move to Winchester. He hadn't realized Merlin had continued working on it.

"Don't get too excited yet," Merlin said. "We still have much work to do to move between realms."

Pip's heart fell, along with his face, but Merlin was quick to continue.

"However, I have made progress. We can now reliably transport a limited number of troops from the Key Stone to any stone circle I specify within this realm."

"So you and Master Bowan . . ." Pip began.

"I received Alfred's message, then Master Bowan and I, along with a select few mages sworn to secrecy, simply walked through the Key Stone and arrived at a stone circle located very close to this spot." Merlin smiled fondly at Alfred. "And I must thank you for that, Alfred. Your mapping of the known stone circles has been extremely helpful in this endeavor."

"Master Merlin," a throaty voice called from the slit of fabric that hung closed at the front of the tent.

"Come," Merlin called.

Ælfstan, the little hobgoblin they'd discovered on the road north, poked his head in through the flaps. "I hope I am not interrupting," he said, pushing through the tent in a way that made his large ears jiggle as they sprang back in place. Ælfstan no longer wore tattered rags but a robe and cloak hemmed to fit him and embroidered with the symbol of the Aurelian Council.

He entered the command tent, securing the tent flaps behind him, then bowed to the group, stopping at Pip. "Master Pip. It is good to see you well. We were concerned," he said, his gravelly voice somewhat softer than before. And stranger still, Pip could understand him without the aid of a spell.

"You speak our language?" Pip's own voice cracked in surprise.

The hobgoblin beamed. At least Pip thought he was beaming. His teeth were gnarly beneath his bulbous nose, but his mouth was twisted upward into a smile. "If I am to be emissary between Faerie and the humans of Britain, then I must speak your language well. Master Alfred has been teaching me."

Alfred blushed. "It has been an honor. And you are an extremely fast learner," Alfred said, then bowed to the small creature.

"What news do you have, Ælfstan?" Bowan asked. "We face a grave threat. Far greater than we first expected. Will your brethren from Faerie help us?"

If the Faerie would help, then surely Pip's power combined with Merlin's, Faerie, and the mages of light would be enough to defeat Halfdan and his demon.

Ælfstan looked about the room, seemingly unsure if he should speak.

"Speak freely, Ælfstan. Those in this room are privy to my counsel and yours," Merlin said. "Just as the mark on your wrist is proof of your loyalty to those who rule Faerie, you, too, have proven your loyalty to us."

Ælfstan nodded. "I have summoned the creatures of Faerie who had come through the weak spots in the wall like me and are also trapped here. They do not wish to be embroiled in human affairs. They only wish to go home."

"We need their numbers," Pip said. Without more fighters, he didn't see how they could win against Halfdan and his warriors—no matter how powerful he and Merlin were together.

"And we cannot send them home until we rid ourselves of the darkness that stands between us and the wall," Bowan said.

"They know this, Master Bowan. They understand the threat the Northmen and the dark mages pose. They see the shroud of darkness this Jarl Halfdan has brought to your lands. They see that if left unattended, these people will bring a great darkness. One that will fill not only your realm, but will also bleed into ours."

Bowan opened his mouth to speak, but Ælfstan raised a hand. "Hear me, Master Bowan. They do not wish to be involved, but as they are trapped here, they see no choice. They will not be ruled by humans. They will not be ruled by Halfdan. We will form our own army. And together we will help protect your realm as well as our own."

"So they'll help us?" Pip asked with relief.

"Yes," said Ælfstan, who then turned to Merlin. "And then I hope that you, Master Merlin, will help those from Faerie return home, if they wish."

Merlin bowed to Ælfstan. "It will be an honor, my friend." Merlin spoke to the group. "And now we make plans for war."

Sixteen

Together they marched north toward Pons Aelius. Gabriella clutched Pip's shoulder firmly, her talons sharp even through the dense fabric of his tunic. He was glad to have her with him—a second set of eyes and ears for the battle to come.

Bowan led a column of battle mages and soldiers on the right, and beside him marched and pranced a motley looking group of creatures the likes of which Pip had never seen. There were several hobgoblins, all of whom had floppy ears, bulbous noses, and gravelly voices like Ælfstan, but the other creatures Alfred had to explain to Pip as they trotted beside them on horseback.

"They've all been in hiding since being trapped here." Alfred looked more excited than he had when Merlin had put him in charge of cataloging King Arthur's old library in preparation for moving it from South Cadbury to Winchester, where the British seat of power would be established. "And I've been tasked with recording everything I can about them! Merlin's even given me a fresh book of parchment to catalog them."

"What's that one then?" Pip asked, looking past the stream of chattering hobgoblins tromping by with Ælfstan in their lead.

"Those are elves," Alfred said, pointing to a small group of graceful human-like creatures who carried the most beautifully crafted bows Pip had ever seen. The yew wood bows were polished and sturdy, and the arrows gleamed gold. Even though his passion for firing arrows had dwindled since the Battle of Badon, those bows were amazing.

Pip watched the elves, male and female, tall and lean and pale. Their auras hummed gold and green like a soft melody on the breeze, almost like Caraline's, but even stronger. Just looking at them made Pip feel happy. It made him long for the times before the world was broken, when he'd run through the forest near his home battling imaginary frights, scavenging for herbs and berries, or chasing Mary around the ancient oak she'd loved so much. He gave a sigh, but it wasn't a sad sigh. For the first time in a long time, he felt happy, warm in the memories.

"Pip. Pip!" Alfred snapped his fingers before Pip's eyes. "Don't stare at the elves too long. Merlin says their auras can be mesmerizing unless they lock them down."

"They seem so peaceful," Pip said, trying to glimpse them from the corner of his eye so their auras were more subdued. "How can they help in battle?"

"That's what I asked, but Ælfstan said they're fearsome fighters when they need to protect the land and their people. They are woodland faeries and fierce protectors of all creatures." Alfred's eyes widened, and he pointed wildly. "Oh, look there! Those must be dwarves! Ælfstan told me about dwarves, but I haven't seen any yet." Reaching for his saddle bag, Alfred couldn't quite unbuckle the clasp. He groaned. "I wish I could write and ride at the same time. Look at them, Pip. Memorize everything you can, and I'll write it all down later."

Pip watched the large band of short, stocky human-like creatures. It was difficult to tell the females from the males except that the male dwarves, so far as Pip could tell, had facial hair and the females didn't. They had thick, muscular bodies, and all carried weapons. Axes. Knives. Shields. Each one wore the finest armor Pip had ever seen.

"Merlin said they've dwelled within the mountains since the Romans pushed their ancestors to the other side of the wall, which is why we've never seen them. Apparently there were dwarves here before the wall was even created, and now other dwarves who were pulled through the weakened wall have joined them. They may wish to stay here or go back. Merlin hasn't met with them yet. But Ælfstan says they're wonderful blacksmiths and warriors."

Warriors. There was that word again. The thing Bowan and Niall thought Pip should be. He just hoped he could prove himself in battle and prevent his friends from being killed.

"What other creatures are there?" Pip asked.

"There are boggarts and pixies. Possibly dragons, but Merlin said they haven't been seen in centuries and could be mere tales."

"What did Ælfstan say about that?" Pip asked.

"Ælfstan's never seen a dragon, but he's heard rumors they exist in Faerie. He does know boggarts and pixies. He said the boggarts, who are marvelous shape-shifters, won't help us at all. He tried to talk them into spying for us, but they refused. Said they'd rather stay living in the moors and marshes of Britain, even under a dark lord, than to help fight a human war. And I think, if we win this, that Ælfstan has a mind to leave them here. So I haven't seen any boggarts yet. Still, I've written down what Ælfstan told me about them." Alfred sighed, then shrugged. "At least the pixies offered to help."

Pip looked around the motley group, searching for some sort of creature Alfred hadn't yet described.

"Oh, you won't see the pixies here." Alfred grinned. "I was lucky enough to visit them with Merlin and Ælfstan last night. They're little wispy creatures with elf-like ears and pale whiteish-green skin and translucent wings."

"They sound so . . . delicate. How can they help?" Pip asked.

"Easy," Alfred said with his usual know-it-all flare. "Pixies like mischief. They readily agreed to help." He leaned sideways from his horse toward Pip and whispered so no one else could hear. "They're planning to gnaw the soles off the shoes of as many of Halfdan Ragnarsson's soldiers as they can before battle." Then he laughed. "Just imagine them tripping over themselves on the field. Perhaps a dark mage will trip and shoot himself with his own spell." Alfred gave a nod of grim satisfaction. "They're supposed to meet us south of the River Tyne to let us know if they've discovered anything useful while destroying the soldiers' shoes."

"Whatever happens," Pip said solemnly, "we mustn't let Halfdan take Mordred's old realm. We've just freed the land from slavery, and we can't allow our people to endure anything like it again."

"Agreed." Alfred nodded. "We're still outnumbered, but with so many Faerie on our side, we will win. We must."

Pip, Alfred, and Gwenn were settled in a patch of tall grass beside the newly erected command tent. The sun was just rising, but the sky hung thick with bruised clouds sizzling with dark power. Gabriella had flown off to the forest's edge for the night, and Pip had yet to see her this morning. He hoped she was well-rested and well-fed.

The British Army and Faerie folk had made camp not far south of the River Tyne. From their vantage point, they could see the previously abandoned Roman fort that sat atop a hill just north of the river. The fortress itself joined with the far east end of Hadrian's Wall, and though not a huge fort, it was imposing compared with the leather tents of the British Army or Halfdan's now abandoned camp.

The ancient fortress had been fortified by Halfdan and his men. A freshly hewn stake wall had been erected around the damaged stone walls, smoke rose from numerous campfires, and the fortress glowed with the auras of dark mages and Northmen.

"Their position will be difficult to breach," Niall said, glancing down at Pip who hadn't realized the big man was there. "Not unless we force them to come to us. Otherwise, they have the advantage."

Gwenn and Pip gazed out at the fortress, while Alfred continued writing in the *Book of Faerie* as he was calling it.

"I suppose that's why the Romans built the fortress on a hillside at the river's edge," Gwenn said. Standing to join Niall, she brushed loose bits of grass from the leather trousers she now wore in place of her usual dress. "It gives them the best position to watch the river and surrounding area."

"Exactly," said Niall. "So we'll have to force them out to meet us before Halfdan regains too much power or summons more strange creatures to do his bidding."

"Perhaps the pixies were successful in their mission," Alfred said, leaping to his feet and pointing to a dark, misty patch of air that approached like a swirl of overly large gnats before landing in an open field near the hobgoblins.

"Perhaps." Merlin appeared beside them like an apparition. "We cannot wait long to draw them out. The wall is weakening, and if it fails, all of Faerie could leak into this realm, including its darkest creatures. Which would cause more chaos—and more opportunity for Halfdan to wreak havoc."

"Merlin." Bowan strode from the command tent, the leather flaps smacking closed behind him. "Are you ready?"

"I am." Merlin gave a grim nod, his eyes sharp like blue ice, then pointed to one of the massive wooden towers the troops had built. It was as tall as the walls of King Arthur's fortress in South Cadbury, except it was on wheels. It could serve as a moving protective wall if they had to abandon their camp, which Pip prayed they wouldn't. "Alfred," Merlin said. "Stay atop the largest siege tower."

The color drained from Alfred's face at the great mage's words. "But I've been practicing with the sword. Haven't I, Niall." Alfred said, looking to the sword master beside him.

"That you have, my boy."

"Then I can fight," Alfred said, putting on the bravest face Pip had ever seen.

"You could, but I suspect you have other skills that will be more useful," said Niall.

"But you need all the fighters you can get," Alfred complained.

"Enough," Merlin barked. "We have no time for bickering or disobedience. You can observe the battle from there. Record all you see." Then he spoke more kindly to Alfred. "If no one writes about the battle, then these events will be lost forever to history. What you do is a vital service to our new realm. Remember that, Alfred."

At those words, Alfred nodded, collected his *Book of Faerie*, a large scroll of parchment, his ink and quills, and dashed off toward a siege tower.

"Gwenn," Merlin said. "Remain in cat form throughout the battle. Infiltrate their camp if possible, but stay away from intense fighting. Learn what you can. If we are defeated, flee with your Aunt Caraline to Winchester. The soldiers remaining there are building a fortress where you should be safe."

"Where is Caraline?" Pip asked.

Merlin pointed to the siege tower across camp. Alfred was just reaching its base. "She will be atop the tower with Alfred. She has been working on a spell to help us."

Finally, Merlin turned to Pip. "Are you ready?"

Pip's stomach dropped like a millstone. He looked from Niall to Bowan to Merlin. He'd shot with his bow under Bowan's strict eye until he'd hit every target dead center without burning anything up. He'd trained for hours and hours with Niall to wield a sword like a battle mage. He'd poured over every grimoire Merlin had given him to study on controlling fire. He'd practiced until his blade held fire without melting. Until he barely had to think to summon fire. But was he ready?

No. He'd never truly be ready, but he realized now that he didn't need to be. The only way he'd prove himself in battle was not to try to *show* Niall or Bowan or Merlin what he could do, but just *do* what he had been practicing. He could control the flames. He hadn't melted another sword. He would use his power on the battlefield just as he'd been practicing, and that would have to be enough. He only hoped *he* would be enough to help defeat Halfdan and survive.

Caw. Caw. Caw. Gabriella let out a series of rapid calls, then swooped down and landed on Pip's shoulder as if to say, *You are enough, and you are not alone.*

"I'm as ready as I can be. I'll do my best to protect the realm." The last bit came out with more confidence because it was true. He hadn't lost his family, helped sever the worlds, and created a new realm only to lose it to another dark mage. And he certainly wasn't about to lose his raven friend either.

"But you." He turned to look at Gabriella. "You must stay out of the fight."

Caw. She complained at him, pecking his ear.

"Ouch. Stop that," he said, rubbing her feathered head affectionately. "I want you to keep an eye on Alfred and the camp. Soar above the fighting and let me know if something is coming that we can't see, but stay out of harm's way."

"Pip's quite right for you to stay safe," said Merlin. "Your ability to see what's coming will be extremely advantageous to us. Be careful of the mages' blasts. They can travel high into the firmament." He spoke seriously to the raven as though she were a fellow mage. "Fly up to Alfred. Show him you're with us. Retreat there if the fighting gets too intense."

Gabriella tilted her head, listening, her black eyes gleaming.

"Do you understand?" Merlin asked the raven, who bobbed her head in response.

"Good." The earth trembled, and the sound of grinding stones echoed from Hadrian's Wall. "It shan't hold much longer. It is time to fight, and then we will repair the wall." Merlin gathered his rowan wood staff in his right hand and straightened to his full height. "Now let us keep this Northman, his dark kin, and the remnants of Mordred's army from staining our lands with darkness once again!"

Merlin nodded to Bowan, who immediately took control. "Swordsmen, at the ready! Archers, take your positions," Bowan's voice boomed over the camp. "Ælfstan," he said, glancing to the hobgoblin who had appeared at Merlin's side. "Command your Faerie folk to do as we discussed."

As the soldiers prepared for battle and the archers took their positions, Bowan took Pip by the elbow. "Pip, lad. I know I've not trained with you since South Cadbury, but your skills are sharp."

"I've been practicing," Pip said, summoning all his courage.

"Good. You have learned to control fire, and with the way you wield the sword ... You'll do well, lad. Besides that, you don't need to worry about joining the archers."

"I—" He still loved the bow, but Pip knew they were keeping him away from the arrows because they were afraid he'd burn their own troops. At least with a sword he could do less harm.

"No, lad," Bowan said with a shake of his head. "It's not your power or control. Niall needs you with Merlin. And we have the elves. Look." Bowan pointed to the siege towers closest to the enemy camp. The elves lined the edges of the towers as if they were ramparts.

Pip's eyes widened as he took in their majestic forms. With their elegant bows drawn and arrows gleaming with ethereal Greek fire, they no longer looked peaceful but fierce.

"Now go with Niall, and I'll see you after the battle." Bowan gave Pip's shoulder a squeeze, and before Pip could say another word, Bowan strode away to issue more orders to the troops. Then, with a loud caw, Gabriella launched herself from Pip's shoulder into the air.

"Stick close to me, lad," Niall said with a spark of eagerness in his eyes. "It'll be just like we practiced. Let's go."

As Niall led Pip to join the line of battle mages and magi-soldiers, the first volley of flaming elven arrows blazed above them like shooting stars. In moments, the wooden palisades of the ancient Roman fort were ablaze.

"For the Magic Realm!" Bowan bellowed, pointing his sword forward from atop his horse. "For Britain!"

Waiting in the cold darkness of the smoky morning haze was torture. The fires burned along the edge of the old Roman fort, and smoke billowed into the air.

The British Army stood ready on the south bank of the River Tyne waiting for their enemy to flee their smoky fortress. The Northmen and dark mages would either attack or defend, but Merlin and Bowan believed mere defense was out of the question for Halfdan. He had come to conquer.

From the stillness, Halfdan's men appeared like specters through the hazy smoke as they poured over the old bridge leading from the fortress across the River Tyne. A few of the men tripped, but others tossed their shoes to the side as if the soleless pieces of leather were a useless burden. Others ran in bare feet. The pixies had succeeded, but it seemed to do little harm to the affected Northmen.

As soon as the dark Northmen were in full view, their battle cries rang out—singing in Pip's ears like banshees wailing for death.

"Sword at the ready," Niall called to Pip. "Channel your power."

Pip drew his sword, his power flowing from his arms and legs and torso into the blade and back again. At the edge of his aura, he could feel Gabriella. She was with Alfred and Caraline at the tower. They were prepared. His body tensed, filling with magic as more elven flames shot overhead, illuminating the sky with trails of green fire. Power shot back from the dark mages, exploding into the British troops in bursts of orange and silver. To Pip's right, Bowan yelled commands.

The hobgoblins drew their long knives and readied their pikes. The dwarves loosed their axes and hammers, swinging them with ease in figure eights, ready to cleave bone. Swords drawn, the mages and magi-soldiers were ready.

"Charge!" Bowan's voice boomed over the armies of Britain and Faerie, and both groups charged the enemy. Spells erupted all around. Steel clashed upon steel.

Pip struck, then parried, then struck again. He was lost in a dance of smoke and blood and magic. He heard nothing but the sounds of clashing swords.

He was separated from Niall when two Northmen set upon him, their muscled arms wielding swords in a strange but deadly manner. Pip charged one, and as he turned to parry the other, a group of pixies swarmed in and yanked the Northman's braided hair and beard so hard they lifted him from his feet. He screamed with shock and rage as the pixies bit his ears and nose while others hauled him backward through the air.

A niggling sensation pulled at Pip, alerting him to Gabriella. She needed him to see something. Eyes on the dark mages and battling Northmen, Pip let his vision blend with the raven's so he could see both the world in front of him and what she intended him to see.

His heart nearly froze, and the hair rose along his arms. Coming across the bridge was Beli. The great horned creature, surrounded by the remnants of Mordred's dark mages, held his arms wide, causing a tidal wave of bodies to part around him as he walked. A dark, twisting umbilical cord of power stretched from the demon to Halfdan Ragnarsson, who fought like a fierce beast, his two blades striking down Britons like massive claws.

An eruption of purple sparks shot up through the smoky battlefield toward the enemy camp, and Pip saw Merlin launch an attack directly at Halfdan and his demon. Merlin was farther back in the fray, but his power traveled faster than Pip could blink. It struck Halfdan in the chest, causing him to stumble, but not fall.

Eyes narrowed, Halfdan aimed his anger toward Merlin, and Pip could sense an immense boiling darkness within the demon. It might even be too much for the great mage to withstand.

"No!" Pip yelled. Yanking his vision back from Gabriella, he swung his sword faster and harder than he'd ever done before. He lost sight of Niall. Of Gabriella. His sole focus was on reaching Halfdan. On stopping him from hurting Merlin.

Pip's blade blazed with light, but the sword held firm. He thrust and parried and thrust again. Men fell, arrows flew, blood soaked the soil, but Pip danced his way over bodies and burning patches of grass in a blinding fury across the smoky battlefield.

Between a gap in the raging Northmen, Pip saw Halfdan Ragnarsson. The jarl fought with swords in each hand, wisps of darkness bleeding from the blades like coiling snakes striking their prey.

"Now!" Halfdan's voice rang out over the clangor, and with a hideous roar, Beli let out a blast of darkness that shot across the field and wrapped itself around Merlin.

"No!" Pip screamed again. Nothing could happen to Merlin. He wouldn't let it. Pip charged Halfdan, all fear and concern over his abilities forgotten. Suddenly Bowan was by his side. Together they slashed and stabbed and chopped. Halfdan's men fell, but more appeared to take their places. If only the troops from the south would arrive.

A deep rumbling laugh issued from behind Pip, making the ground tremble and his teeth vibrate. Pip turned to find he stood in the hazy shadow of Beli.

With gnarly teeth, the demon grinned. Holding a strand of darkness in the air, he revealed Merlin screaming in fiery pain, trapped in a noose-like sack of smoke. The old wizard tore and ripped at his cage, but his spells fell uselessly at his feet.

Bowan roared with rage, striking at the demon's foot, but he was tossed aside with a twitch of the great beast's hand. "Take care of him, Halfdan. I'll take the boy." The voice was deep, merciless, inhuman.

At that moment, everything seemed to slow. Pip saw the bloodied bodies of hobgoblins and pixies and elves. The bodies of his own soldiers broken, trampled. Merlin trapped and in pain. No more soldiers were coming. Not in time to help. This was it. If Pip did not defeat this demon and the Northmen, all would be lost.

When Halfdan's sword clashed with Bowan's, the sharp sound pierced the air, and magic erupted from each blade. The dark Northman charged Bowan, his power fortified by the beast. Pip stepped toward his mentor, but a fiery horned tail smashed into the earth in front of him.

"Your friend will die, boy. And if you refuse to ally yourself with Halfdan Ragnarsson, so will you." Beli's tail swept toward Pip, causing the ground to tremble.

Pip leapt over the spiked tail, then ducked beneath the creature's bony claw as if he were running a gauntlet. Pip summoned his power, drawing what he could from the earth and wind as well as the fire, but the demon was fast. A spell rumbled from Beli's gnarled throat, catapulting fire toward Pip, who tucked and rolled away from the blazing blast.

Pip spotted a large boulder close to the river. Dodging another blast, he ducked behind the rock just in time to feel its surface flare with heat. Edging around the far side of the boulder, Pip spied Bowan. On his knees. Halfdan's sword plunging into his chest.

Bowan's eyes went wide. His sword fell from his bloodied hand, and his eyes fluttered up to heaven.

"No!" Pip screamed. Rage flooded his veins. It mingled with the earth and wind, with the demon fire and the river water. All the power surged inside him, erasing any fear or pain. His mind focused to a sharp point, and pure, raw *draoidheachd* poured into him.

His energy surged. All his anger and pain and power were focused on Beli. "Bàs!" Pip screamed the old word his da had used for death, and like a banshee hungry for destruction, he charged toward Halfdan and the demon. Pip was a tidal wave of magic flooding toward the demon.

The Northmen soldiers and dark mages in his path turned to dust, and the great wave of power flowing from Pip coursed over Beli, forcing him to stagger, then fall to his knees. His grasp on Merlin's smoky cage loosened, then released. Merlin dropped to the ground, unmoving, but still Pip charged.

"Beli!" Halfdan yelled, clinging to the one sword he still held.

The demon struggled to rise, but invisible tendrils of power held him to the earth. Pip turned to Halfdan Ragnarsson.

Pip slashed his fiery sword with all his muscle and power and magic at Halfdan.

Their swords clashed, and the jolt rang out like thunder that splits the heavens. Light burst from Pip's sword, disintegrating its blade, but also splitting Halfdan's weapon in two, leaving only a jagged fragment in his hand.

As their swords broke, a ripple of green power shot across the battlefield from the tower where Caraline stood with hands outstretched. The earth shook. The soldiers staggered in the earthquake, and a huge fissure opened in the ground like a great mouth, revealing smoldering fires. Beli roared. He struggled to free himself from his invisible bonds, but by some unseen force within the earth, he was yanked deep into the flames.

Halfdan screamed in agony, his essence ripping as his aura separated from the demon, who disappeared into the bowels of the earth. Then a rumbling, grinding sound rang out like a million stones of ice falling in winter. Pip and all those on the battlefield turned to look just beyond the river.

A great hole tore open in Hadrian's Wall, and the strange energy of Faerie bled through. Rays of green and gold and gray seeped into the world. Creatures crept through like insects, and a sudden *screech* made them all look skyward.

A massive creature with leathery wings and pearlescent black scales shot through the rip in the wall. *A dragon?* Pip marveled.

The dragon screeched again, and Pip's heart twinged with panic. *Gabriella.* Pip reached out to her with his mind and felt the familiar tug. *Get out of the sky.*

Pip saw the great winged creature through Gabriella's eyes, feeling both her fear and awe of the giant flying beast.

Screech! The dragon swooped from overhead, snapping up a dark mage in his maw.

Stay down. Near camp. Protect Alfred and Caraline. Be safe, Pip commanded. Gabriella bristled at his tone. *Please. Bowan is dead. Maybe Merlin. I can't lose you, too.*

Caw. Gabriella called out her sorrowful understanding and turned toward camp, severing her shared vision with Pip.

The ground continued to tremble, and Pip staggered to Merlin's side. The great mage was extremely pale, and smoke issued from his beard. He lay motionless, except for his fingers that skimmed the river's surface.

"Merlin!" Pip cried, collapsing next to him. Pip willed all of his power into the healing spell he'd learned so long ago, then released it into the great mage. Merlin gave a soft moan. His eyes fluttered open, then rolled up in his sockets as he took a long, raspy breath, then fell silent.

"Merlin!" Pip shook the mage, but there was no response. "Merlin!" But Merlin stirred no more.

Pip tilted his head back and screamed. But his scream was more than a scream. It was a scream filled with raw power. A scream filled with all of the fear and agony and loss he'd ever known. Of losing his mother and sister, his brother and father. Of losing Bowan and Merlin. Of losing his home. How much loss could one heart bear?

As the last note of Pip's wail died on the air, the world fell silent. The ground stopped quaking. Creatures stopped flooding through the wall. The fighting stopped. All eyes were upon him, except for Halfdan, who still lay writhing near the place in the earth where Beli had disappeared.

Pip heaved. The triskele mark on his palm grew warm and glowed with orange and golden light. The triskele's warmth spread up his arm until his whole being was illuminated by fiery gold with the strength and power that signified both a fire mage and a battle mage. And on his bloodied red sash, two runes appeared: the rune symbol for fire in blazing orange and the rune symbol for warrior gold.

He'd done it. He had mastered the power required to be a fire mage and a battle mage.

But what good was being a fire mage and battle mage if he'd lost those he loved most? What did it matter if he saved the realm and its people? Without those he loved, his life was meaningless.

He bowed his head over Merlin and wept.

Seventeen

"Why do you weep?" An ethereal, feminine voice broke the silence.

Pip lifted his face toward the sound and was nearly blinded by the white light that spilled from the wound-like gap in the wall and flowed out to blanket the river's surface. The light embraced him like a gentle hug, then dimmed so he could see clearly.

From the river, a pale woman with fine features and dark hair emerged. She wore a gossamer gown of glistening silver that seemed to be made of mist. She took hold of Merlin's hand, which lay in the water, and held it gently as she came to his side.

"Who—who are you?" Pip asked, finding his voice through his tears. He'd never seen a woman so powerful or so beautiful. She seemed neither young nor old, neither sister nor mother—but a timeless power who could enchant his heart. Any soldiers, light or dark, who had yet to lay down their weapons did so now. Then all on the battlefield knelt before her.

The lady smiled down at Pip kindly. "I am not for you, young Pip." She whispered some words in a strange tongue, and the enchantment Pip had felt for the lady fell away like cobwebs from his eyes. She was still beautiful and powerful, but he no longer felt taken by her beauty.

"I am Nimuë. The Lady of the Lake," she said. "A friend of Merlin's. I look kindly upon both human and Faerie—most of the time."

"Can you help him? I've tried, but . . . please, help him."

"Perhaps." She closed her eyes and squeezed Merlin's hand gently before opening them again. "He has not yet reached Death's border. I can help him, and I will help you as well, young Pip. Your heart is true, and you have more yet to do for this new kingdom than you know." She closed her eyes again, and the white light that had announced the lady's arrival again grew so intense that Pip could not see. But he could feel it. Tendrils of light lapped at his skin, dancing with his power as it seeped into Merlin. Pip felt it clean the smoke and ash from Merlin's skin and hair and lungs. Felt it clean away the damage that Halfdan Ragnarsson and Beli had wrought.

As quickly as it had appeared, the light retreated. And when Pip blinked, the light and the lady were gone.

Merlin sat up, blue eyes blinking, his beard and hair as white as snow. "Nimuë?"

"You are healed, my friend. And your apprentice is given a chance to become all he is meant to be." Her voice echoed through the large fissure in the wall and out over the water's surface. "Behold the sword in the stone."

A grinding sound caused Pip to twist around so he could see the large boulder he'd used as cover when he'd fought Beli. A radiant light beamed down upon the stone, and in its center appeared a massive sword.

"I give you Caliburn," said Nimuë. "It's sister, Excalibur, is with King Arthur in another realm. The two swords shall always be kindred, just as your two realms are kindred, but they shall be wielded by separate kings. He who draws Caliburn from this stone shall rule all of Britain in this realm, as Arthur rules the other."

The steel of the sword's blade gleamed in the lady's light. Its pommel was wrought with gold and encrusted with a blood-red ruby, but the blade was sharp and sang of death.

Before Pip could fully appreciate the sword's splendor, Halfdan Ragnarsson, bloody and battle weary, leapt upon the boulder. "I shall be king!" Halfdan gripped the hilt, and he yanked with all his Northman strength. Yet it was as if the sword had been plastered permanently in place. It did not move.

A rush of power surged through Pip, urging him to his feet. In a moment, he, too, stood atop the stone. "Stay back!" Pip called, feeling the energy of a new battle mage blaze through his blood. A blast of power shot from Pip's hand, knocking Halfdan off the stone and onto the ground.

Before Halfdan could find his feet, Pip took hold of the sword's grip, and at that moment, everything became one. It wasn't his power or his control that had been wrong. It had been his weapon. He had not found a sword that could wield his power—until now.

His aura joined with the sword just as it had joined with Gabriella. He could feel the sword's aura sing in his blood. It was connected to the earth of the Magic Realm and that of Faerie, but also tied to the Earth Realm and King Arthur through its sister sword, Excalibur. Somehow it made sense that no other sword had felt right in his hands. None of those swords had been meant for him. None of them could contain his power. This one could.

In his grasp, the sword loosed from the stone and slid like a knife through lard on a warm summer day. It was as if the earth had heaved a great sigh. The sword was free in his hand.

Sword raised before him, Pip looked at those who stood around him. Merlin was on his feet now, his blue eyes sparkling with pride. Niall was the first to kneel, then the other soldiers of light followed.

Pip shook his head, gesturing for them to rise. "Don't kneel for me! I am a mage—a battle mage—I am not a king." He pointed the sword toward Halfdan and his dark army, who were now retreating over the bridge and disappearing behind the fortress walls. "Stop the Northman and his dark army! Stop them now, before they refortify the fortress!"

"Do as he says!" Merlin bellowed, raising his staff and shooting a bolt of lightning from its end.

In a blink, the British soldiers were on their feet, stopping whatever dark soldiers they could find—yet most had already fled to the safety of the fortress.

Caliburn in hand, Pip leapt down from the stone. "We should drive them out," he said. "We must end this while we still can."

"There are more pressing matters to which we must attend." Merlin pointed his staff toward the gaping hole in Hadrian's Wall, which now bled more creatures. "It appears Nimuë's spell has broken. We must first stop the flow of creatures from Faerie, then return our attention to Halfdan. With Beli gone, he is weakened. We should combine our powers to reinforce the wall. If we can contain the creatures behind it, then we can recount our numbers and devise a new plan."

Pip longed to chase the last of the dark mages and Northmen across the bridge, but Merlin was right. The troops from the south would arrive and refortify them. They'd lost too many to attack now. Pip ground his teeth in frustration as he watched the last of their enemy disappear into the fortress. The portcullis ground closed with a rusty thud, and a dark shield of power billowed out like a massive storm cloud, encircling the old stone walls, protecting those within.

"It will take our renewed strength to breach the walls," Niall said, coming up beside Pip and Merlin. "And we've lost many men. Bowan. . ."

"He will be buried in a warrior's grave," Merlin said, his eyes softening.

Pip's heart stung as he gazed at the fallen form of the warrior who had first saved him from the slavers and then from doubting himself. Bowan. Who had forced him to become better, even when he thought he couldn't.

"And yet we are still strong." Caraline, her face stained with earth and tears, approached them with Alfred and Gwenn on either side. Gabriella swooped in a circle above them, then dove and landed on Pip's shoulder, giving him a little caw and a nibble.

"Caraline." Merlin embraced her. "I feared for your safety."

"And I for yours, Merlin," she said, returning his embrace.

"We saw everything." Alfred's eyes sparkled wildly, and Pip noticed his fingers were stained black with ink. "When the wave of power shot from you, Pip, that's when Caraline did her spell. You should have seen her."

"Alfred said that Aunt Caraline used the demon's name and cast the spell that made the ground tremor and the soldiers quake," Gwenn said with pride.

"Together you caused Beli to be sucked back to Hell," Alfred said. "I've recorded it all, but I'll go back and make further annotations later once I speak to those from the battlefield. I will record their accounts."

"Well done," Merlin said to each in turn. Then he called out to all who remained standing around them. "Gather the mages and magi alike. Together we will reinforce the wall."

They stood in a line. Soldiers. Mages. Hobgoblins. Dwarves. Elves. Pixies. All who had survived Mordred's rule and Halfdan's wrath. All who stood for the light. Together they faced the gaping hole in Hadrian's Wall.

Hands held out before them, each summoned their power. The farmers, shopkeepers, other magus, and Alfred glowed faintly of orange and white, yellow and green. The energy of the soldiers and mages shone more brightly in the same hues but also in silver and purple and gold.

Merlin stood in the center of them all with Pip, Alfred, and Ælfstan to his right, Caraline, Gwenn, and Niall to his left. When the line of Britons hummed with power, Merlin spoke.

"Any of Faerie blood who stand with us and wish to return, go now!" Merlin commanded, his voice echoing like a god over the field and into the sky. "Add your power to the wall from the other side. Once it is resealed, you will be unable to return."

A flurry of creatures broke from the line. Hobgoblins. Pixies. Dwarves. Elves. But not all of them. Some from each race stayed, standing strong with their human companions, including Ælfstan, who kept his place beside Alfred.

"Don't you want to go home?" Alfred asked the hobgoblin.

Pip saw an uncertain look on the hobgoblin, but then his bumpy face broke into a grin. "No, Master Alfred. I was a mere wall guardian in Faerie. Here, I am more. I will help you catalogue those Faerie who remain here and continue teaching you and Mistress Gwenn how to speak my language. I will stay, if you'll have me."

Alfred's murmur of power faltered, but he held his hands forward, and his aura brightened. "Of course I'll have you, Ælfstan. I would hug you right now if I could."

Pip nearly laughed at the thought of Alfred's tall, lanky form embracing Ælfstan's squat awkward one. He was glad the hobgoblin was here. Ælfstan spoke many languages, and his power was strong.

After the flurry of creatures scampering back through the wall subsided, Merlin's hands glowed blindingly white. "When I speak the incantation, everyone must release your power at the wall. Imagine it going into mortar, into stone. Sealing off our realm from that of Faerie. We want nothing dark to come through."

Pip focused his power, thinking of the triskele on his left hand and the immense power he felt at being a battle mage. His hands and arms glowed brighter, and the energy surged through his body until he could see nothing but golden white light.

He felt, rather than heard, Merlin's incantation. It was as if a great dam had broken and the power of sound and light flooded from him and everyone around him, crashing like a tidal wave into the wall. Then there was silence.

Where the hole had been was a herringbone pattern of golden light that held the wall together, and the hum of magic slowly faded and settled into the ether.

"Let what has been done never be undone," said Ælfstan to all who stood together. "And those of us who have chosen to stay behind will make this our home. We shall protect the Magic Realm and all those of light who live here."

Eighteen

With Gabriella riding atop Pip's shoulder and Caliburn sheathed in a leather scabbard at his side, Pip truly felt like a battle mage. He'd fought another hardened mage and a demon and won. And now he had a sword that he knew he couldn't destroy. The sword he'd pulled from the stone, Caliburn, somehow felt part of him—its weight and balance perfect, its energy aligned with his. Its blade sang of death, but the sword itself was an instrument of peace. And Pip would wield it to help Merlin bring peace to the land and the people.

It thumped comfortingly against his leg as he walked beside Merlin, leading the remains of their tattered army back to Eoforwic. It would take four days to reach the fortress there; then Merlin would travel via stone portal to Winchester to check on the progress of the new castle. In the meantime, their wounded would recover, the troops from the south would arrive, scouts would scour the land for more soldiers, and they would plan for what to do about Halfdan Ragnarsson and his dark army who remained sheathed behind the Fortress of Darkness, as Alfred called it, at the edge of Hadrian's Wall.

"At least Halfdan will receive no aid from dark creatures of Faerie," Pip said. "Nor can he draw upon their power."

"That is something," Merlin said, seemingly lost in thought. "But there is still the matter of having a ruler in place to quell unrest across the land. You heard Nimuë. She is a powerful sorceress. He who draws Caliburn from this stone shall rule all of Britain in this realm. And you pulled—"

"Yes. I pulled the sword from the stone, but I'm no ruler, Merlin. I'm definitely not a king. I grew up on a small plot of land with a garden and had to hunt for meat."

"Great rulers have risen from lesser means."

Pip scowled. "Is it not enough that I'm a battle mage? It's what you and . . . it's what you and Bowan wanted. I've done it. I'll use this sword and serve our new kingdom, but I don't know the first thing about ruling. Surely one of King Arthur's mage lords can do it?"

"I'll speak with them when I visit Winchester, and I won't press you on the matter—for now." The edges of Merlin's lips twisted in a small smile, which Pip knew meant he would be hearing more about this king business. "For now, we will rest and recover at Eoforwic. We have quelled, even if temporarily, the dangers from the Northmen, and Hadrian's Wall has been reinforced. We shall take stock of what Faerie creatures now reside here and come up with a plan. Then, one day soon, we will take the north from the dark, and our new realm will finally come under the dominion of one ruler. The one true king."

"Well, that won't be me," Pip said and walked ahead to be with Alfred and Gwenn, who were laughing. He had already accomplished all that he had set his mind to, far more than he ever imagined. He'd come a long way from his small home in the north: from being a boy with hidden power to an apprentice to a full-blown battle mage. He didn't want or need a crown. Despite the nettle-like sting of missing his sister and father and brother, he had all he needed right here. He had Merlin and Caraline, Alfred and Gwenn. They were his family now, and they would always be with him.

Glossary

Albion: The earliest known name for Britain, likely given to the island because of its white chalky cliffs.

Arrow slit window: An arrow slit, also known as an arrow loop, is a narrow, vertical opening in a fortification through which an archer can shoot arrows or a crossbowman can shoot bolts.

Aura: The energy field of any living thing or an extremely powerful magical object. It can be seen by mages as different colors surrounding a person; these colors may change depending on a person's mood or health. The stronger the mage, the better they can see an aura.

Aurelian Council of Mages: The newly formed council appointed by Merlin to rule Britain after the fall of Mordred.

Battle mage: Born magus and trained as a mage. The battle mage specializes in battle magic. They wear the red sash of a mage with gold runes of the battle mage.

Blót: An old Norse term for blood sacrifice.

Boggart: A shape-shifting creature from English folklore. Boggarts tend to live alone and reside on moors or in marshes.

The Breaking: The ripping apart of the ordinarius, or non-magical humans, and the magus, or magical humans, so each population could live in their own separate realms on Earth. This occurred circa 500 A.D.

Caledonian Forest: An ancient pine forest in Scotland. The modern pines are direct descendants of the pines first introduced to the region around 7,000 B.C.

Cat sìth: Fairy cats of Celtic mythology. These cats can be as large as dogs and are believed to transform between cats and witches and back again.

Draoidheachd (*droy-yee-uch-k*): The Scottish Gaelic word for sorcery or magic.

Draugr: The spirit of a Viking who was so greedy in life that would sometimes come back and haunt the living for treasure.

Druid: Religious leaders among the ancient Celts; some believe they were sorcerers or magicians.

Dwarf: A short, stocky human-like creature. Dwarves excel in metalwork and typically live underground.

Elf: An elegant, human-like creature with ethereal beauty that extends beyond themselves and into their auras. Elves have powerful magic and are deeply connected to the earth.

Faerie: The Gaelic word for fairy.

Freyja: The Norse goddess of fate, love, beauty, war, and fertility.

Goblin: An ugly, knobby humanoid creature that is short in stature. They are malevolent and prefer to work with creatures of the dark. They tend to live in caverns and shallow caves.

Gothi: A pagan priest; minister of the Norse gods.

Green sash: Worn by those who are magus to show they have supernatural abilities.

Grimoire: A book of magic

Hadrian's Wall: A Roman wall built under the direction of the Emperor Hadrian beginning in 122 A.D. to keep back the northern tribes of Britain.

Hardtack: A saltless hard biscuit or bread. Common food for soldiers when on the move because it was easy to store and quick to eat.

Hobgoblin: Similar in appearance to the goblin, except slightly shorter, hobgoblins prefer mischief to malevolence and align themselves with creatures of the light.

Imbolc: A traditional Gaelic festival that marks the beginning of spring.

Jarl: A Norse chief.

Loki: A trickster god in Norse mythology who has the ability to shape-shift; he is father to three monsters: Fenrir, the wolf; Jörmungandr, the serpent; and Hel, a giantess who rules over one of the Viking underworlds.

Magus (*plural magi*): A person born with magical abilities.

Magus-priest: Born magus and trained as a priest, but not powerful enough to achieve the status of full mage. They wear a green sash with holy symbols of both the Christians and the druids.

Magus-soldier: Born magus and trained as a soldier, but not powerful enough to achieve the status of a full mage or battle mage. They wear a green sash with silver runes.

Niflheim: A cold, dark, misty realm of the dead in Norse mythology.

Odin: One of the most powerful and honored gods of the Norse. The god of death, divination, and magic in Norse mythology.

Order of Mages: A group of powerful mages that oversees the training and appointment of other mages, as well as the use of magic throughout the kingdom.

Pixie: Tiny elf-like creatures with wings with a penchant for mischief. They typically live in groups on moorlands.

Red sash: Worn by a magus who has attained the status of full mage.

Scriptorium: A writing room in a monastery where scribes copied manuscripts.

Sìth: Gaelic word for fairy.

Stone circles: A circular alignment of stones. The earliest of these structures appeared around 5,000 B.C.

Thor: The Norse god of lightning, thunder, storms, strength, and protection.

Thrall: A slave or servant to the Vikings; sometimes they were enslaved as prisoners of war.

Triskele: An ancient Celtic symbol. The original meaning of the symbol is unknown, but it is believed to hold the power of three.

Wattle and daub: A traditional building method in which interwoven sticks and twigs are covered with clay, mud, soil, and animal dung.

Winter solstice: This solstice marks the beginning of winter and is the shortest day of the year.

Author's Note

Balancing history while writing fantasy can be challenging. My endeavor was to creatively embrace historical truths of the early British peoples, both druid and Christian, along with the Northmen. I created my own historical timeline, greatly simplified geopolitical Britain of the period, and had the Vikings invade England well before the Viking Age actually began. It is possible that the Northmen were aware of England and its politics and society before the beginning of the historic Viking Age, which began on 8 June 793 when a Viking raiding party despoiled the monastery at Lindisfarne in northeast England.

Writing about people who lived so long ago allowed me vast creative freedom because we simply don't have all of the historic evidence to prove exactly what happened and when. For instance, when and where did King Arthur live and die? Was he, in fact, one person or a combination of heroes? There are also questions about the specifics of Merlin and the Vikings.

Merlin was a historic figure, likely a druid, but he was probably alive after the Battle of Badon. The legend of King Arthur may be inspired by Ambrosius Aurelianus, the Celtic hero and war leader closely tied with Merlin the Wizard. Geoffrey of Monmouth (c. 1095–1155) chronicled historical and legendary figures of Britain and seems to have combined people and tales to create the figure of Merlin Ambrosius. Although some historians say Merlin was likely not connected to Ambrosius Aurelianus, I chose to pay tribute to this old and popular tale by naming Merlin's council the Aurelian Council of Mages in this book.

As evidence from the past is still being uncovered, we're learning more about not only Merlin and the legendary King Arthur, but also about when the Vikings, or Northmen, first ventured far from their Scandinavian homes. While some future discoveries may prove inaccuracies in any history I've included here, please know I did purposely blend history with fantasy for the sake of storytelling.

All that said, it was my intent to take basic ideas that formed these people's religious and cultural perspectives and bring them together in a clash of beliefs and ideologies to create a powerful and engaging fantasy world. I hope the bits of history I have interwoven will capture readers' imaginations and urge them to learn more about these amazing people, their travels, their ideas, and their histories.

To research this book, I read numerous articles on the legend of King Arthur and Merlin, and on creatures from British folklore. To immerse myself in the world of the Vikings and early medieval England, I rewatched the television series *Vikings, The Last Kingdom,* and *Vikings Valhalla*. I also did an immense amount of research. If you'd like to learn more, here are some places, articles, and websites I found particularly helpful.

During my time living in England, I found York Minster Library, York Castle Museum, the JORVIK Viking Centre, and the Tower of London to be invaluable resources. I read many articles online, but the articles I found particularly helpful were translations of "The Welsh Triads" from the Celtic Literature Collective; "Timeline of Roman Britain" by Ben Johnson on historic-uk.com; "The Battle of Mount Badon" by J.A. Canon from www.encyclopedia.com; "The Vikings in Britain: a Brief History" (2011) on history.org.uk; "The First Vikings" (2013) by Andrew Curry in *Archaeology* magazine; articles by Dr. Caitlin R. Green on caitlingreen.org, including her article "Anglo-Saxon or sub-Roman: what should we call Lincolnshire in the fifth and sixth centuries?" (2015); "What Did the Vikings Look Like" (2018) on www.skjalden.com; "Lindisfarne: The 'Holy Island' where Vikings

Spilled the 'blood of saints'" (2020) by Owen Jarus on livescience.com; and "In 793 AD the Vikings Attacked Lindisfarne" (2022) by Alec Marsh on nationalgeographic.co.uk. I also found medievalchronicles.com a useful resource. There are so many other sites I visited, but this is a list of those that helped me bring authenticity to my tale.

Acknowledgments

Thank you so much, readers, for reading this twist on the legend of Merlin and Arthur and for following Pip on his adventure. The Arthurian legend and this period of British history have fascinated me for most of my life, and I was excited to couple my fascination with fantasy and historic research. I truly hope you have enjoyed it!

I must also thank my amazing editor, Deborah Halverson, who continues to encourage me through my writing journey. Thank you to Cat Scully for the phenomenal map. Thanks also to the cover artist, Christian Bentulan, for his beautiful work.

Thank you to my Scottish friend, Lawrence Crawford, for double-checking my use of Gaelic in the *Merlin's Apprentice* series. Thank you to my friend and grammar guru, Pat Cuchens, for giving this book a final pass and input before it went to press. And thanks to all of my family and friends who have believed in me and my writing over the years.

Finally, thank you to my mother, Sandy Basso, who reads and gives me feedback on everything I write. And last, but certainly not least, thank you to my husband, Rick, and my son, Alex, who have supported me through the trials of the writing process, have had patience when I had to write despite them wanting me to do something else, and have given me their endless love and support.

Also by Susan McCauley

Merlin's Apprentice: The Mage (Book 1)

The Devil's Tree

The Demon Tailor

Ghost Hunters: Bones in the Wall (Book 1)

Ghost Hunters: Pirates' Curse (Book 2)

Ghost Hunters: Spirit Fire (Book 3)

Ghost Hunters: Swamp Witch (Book 4)

Milton Keynes UK
Ingram Content Group UK Ltd.
UKHW032330041024
449133UK00013B/177/J